The Retreat
Helen Vivienne Fletcher

For Hana, who encouraged me to write this way back
when.

Chapter One

Dad didn't notice that I was giving him the silent treatment. He chattered away from the driver's seat, perhaps mistaking my lack of response for rapt interest in his lecture on the merits of this cult he was dragging us off to. Of course, he didn't call it a cult. It was "The Retreat", and as always it was said with a forced serene sigh on the second e.

When we stopped for lunch, he picked out two salad sandwiches for us. Before the accident, he loved taking us out for lunch – *choose anything* he'd say, with an expansive wave of his hand. Now I couldn't even pick my own sandwich filling.

I added a coke to the tray.

The manic smile Dad had been wearing since stuffing our lives into the boot of the car finally dropped. "They don't allow refined sugar at The Retreat," he said. He reached for the bottle, but I closed my hand around it.

"We're not at The Retreat yet."

I tried to hold his eye, but he looked away and ran his hand down the sides of his chin, nervously pulling at his beard. I figured that meant I could have the coke.

Dad was a physicist back in our real lives. I know; not the type of guy you'd expect to run off to a "retreat". My little sister always used to pronounce it "fiss-hiss-sis" which was equal parts endearing and annoying. I think that was part of why Dad quit his job and dragged us off – so he didn't have to be reminded every time someone lisped their way through his job title.

I took a deep breath and shook my head to clear it. I didn't want to be reminded either.

We munched our way through a silent lunch, then trudged back to the car. Dad slid into the driver's seat, his lips stretching out into that disturbing grin again.

How many days had we been on the road? Time was becoming meaningless in the void of continuous car noise. The only indication of how long we'd been away was the flush of red blooming on the back of Dad's forearms. My own arms had just gone from brown to browner since I take after Mum, rather than Dad's pastiness. She would have reminded him to put sunscreen on. I let him burn.

"Have I ever told you about Schrödinger's cat, Finn?" Dad flicked on the indicator, taking us back out onto another stretch of paddock-lined road. I welcomed the sight of the asphalt, knowing the roar of the tyres rushing over it would soon drown Dad out.

He didn't wait for an answer, launching into the story of how some nutbar thought putting a cat in a box with poison and a bunch of radioactive crap was a good way to prove something. Dad had explained the dead-not-dead cat to me before, but he obviously didn't remember. I could tell where he was going with this. Once he thought he'd captured me in wonderment, thinking about the fact that the cat was both alive and dead, he'd spring some lame parallel on me about how our old life and our new life at The Retreat were both alive and dead at the same time. Then he probably thought we'd hug.

"So, the cat is a zombie?" I took a sip from the bottle of coke and watched as he struggled to dig his way out of that one.

"No... it's not alive *and* dead, it's just you can think of it as both." His forehead puckered up, seemingly frustrated at my general lack of enlightenment.

I turned my face away, staring out of the window. "Sounds like a zombie to me."

Dad fell into a merciful silence.

YOU HAVE TO GET OUT...
... Go get help, Finn.
You have to get out... Finn... Finn...

"FINN... FINN!" DAD opened my car door, letting in a rush of cool air. I startled awake.

You have to get out... My chest squeezed tight, threatening to suffocate me. I swallowed hard, closing my eyes.

When I used to fall asleep in Mum's car, she always woke me by mussing the too-long-in-her-opinion curls on the top of my head. Dad didn't touch me. He just called my name over and over until I hauled my ass out of the car to make him stop.

The afternoon sun cast peachy orange bands across the hills as it snuck lower behind them. We were in a small, dirt carpark on the side of the road. Several cars stood stationary between the faded white lines, but they were covered in dust, bird shit and other miscellaneous crap, like they'd been left there for months if not years. There were no buildings in sight, only bush and trees stretching out around us.

Dad took our bags from the back, then closed the car door behind him, locking it.

"Dad, where are we?"

"At The Retreat." Dad's manic grin stretched, practically dislocating his jaw.

This was... concerning. I knew he was having some kind of breakdown, dragging us off to this weirdo place, but what if The Retreat didn't even exist? Were we about to go bush, living off the land in the middle of nowhere until we either perished out here or Dad came to his senses? My money was on perish, given that between the two of us we had approximately zero survival skills.

"We have to walk the last part of the journey," he said. "It's symbolic."

Symbolic, my ass. Sounded like The Retreat just wanted to stay hidden, so no one called them on their kooky bullshit.

Dad picked up his bag, then took off down a barely visible path. I looked between him and the car. He had the keys, but surely I could hotwire it or something? I mean... I wasn't entirely sure what hotwiring was, which was a bit of a barrier. I also wasn't sure if you could hotwire modern cars. Damn my lack of mechanical knowledge!

Dad disappeared into the bush, and the tightly packed trees seemed to swallow him.

"Dad, wait up!" I took one last longing look at the car, then raced after him.

I WASN'T GREAT AT JUDGING distance, but it felt like we walked at least a couple of kilometres. The bush grew denser and the path narrower, until I could barely see it.

"Dad, are you sure we're going the right way?"

Dad didn't slow his pace, but he frowned, showing some hesitation for the first time since we started this trek. "I... think so?"

"You have found the right path," a voice called from somewhere behind the tangle of leaves. A tall, solidly built figure stepped forward, parting the branches.

I stared. The man was clad head to toe in some sort of loose muslin wrap, like a cross between an ill-fitting bathrobe and bad Princess Leia cosplay. I really hoped this was a fashion statement and not a sign of things to come.

He reached out, taking Dad's hands. "I am glad you have arrived safely."

Dad beamed, but I scowled at the man. He eyed our bags, frowning. He probably thought we were going to ask him to help carry them, but he didn't need to worry. My pack was the only link I had left to home, and I wasn't letting go of it.

"Come," the man said, his voice gentle. "I will guide you safely on the rest of your journey."

He turned, disappearing into the trees almost instantly. I looked back the way we'd come. My chances of finding the carpark alone seemed slim at best, and as already mentioned, I had little to no basic survival skills. I begrudgingly followed after Dad.

We walked I'm guessing another kilometre or two before we broke through the trees into a clearing. The Retreat stood in front of us, silhouetted by the setting sun.

Whatever I'd been picturing, this was not it. A collection of buildings, like a school campus filled the large clearing. Four multistorey wooden buildings marked the centre, then a collection of smaller structures and cabins spread out in a circle around them. Towering fences caged the whole compound.

How many people lived here? I'd been picturing The Retreat as a group of twenty or so flaky weirdos living in tents, but this place was big enough to house several hundred flaky weirdos.

People milled around the grounds, doing what looked like farm tasks – digging and planting seedlings, gathering baskets of vegetables. Every single one of them was wrapped in lengths of pastel-coloured muslin.

Perhaps I understated the weirdness earlier. That first man we met? Definitely not a fashion statement. The floaty wraps wound all around them, including over their heads, so they looked like they were wearing loose hoods. And Dad insisted this wasn't a cult.

"Dad, seriously, what the...?" I stopped just short of swearing. Somehow, I didn't think that would go down too well here.

The way they were swathed in fabric, it was hard to tell who they were – age, gender, race, it all blurred into one. I guess that could be a good thing – one way to thwart all the -isms – but unease crept over me at not being able to tell them apart. I searched for clues like height, and the occasional hint of curves, but I could have been standing in a crowd of clones.

One of the figures looked up as my eyes traced over them. A girl, definitely. She met my eye through the folds of pale-green muslin looping her face. Even with the distance and the fence between us, I could tell she had wide inky-dark brown eyes, almost black, just like Mum's had been. Just like mine. Her gaze fixed on me intensely, the type of look that half drew me in, half made me want to shrink down to the ground and squirm like some pathetic toddler.

I looked away, desperate to focus on anything else.

One of the muslin-clad men unlocked a gate, beckoning for us to come through it. "Welcome," he said. "Mother is waiting for you."

I sincerely hoped that the woman he was referring to was actually biologically related to him. That was going to be one hell of a step too far down the bullshit road if not.

He led us through the vegetable-growing area into one of the four buildings in the centre of the compound. *They better not be expecting us to help with the vegetables.* Dad could kill a pot plant just by looking at it.

Things seemed more normal inside. Warm, creamy coloured walls and bright macramé wall hangings greeted us, making the space feel almost welcoming. If I hadn't seen the fences surrounding the property, I could have convinced myself we were walking into the foyer of a meditation class, or an alternative backpackers' hostel. Then I caught sight of another of those swaddled, pastel-coloured shapeless people, and my stomach clenched.

The man reached for our bags.

"I can carry it," I said, not letting go of the strap.

The man smiled. "We do not bring outside possessions into Mother's room."

I... did not know how to argue with a statement as weird as that. I let go of the bag.

A short, round woman came forward to grip my hand. No loop of fabric covered her head indoors, but lengths circled her body, exaggerating the roundness. She wasn't overweight, not exactly, but she seemed to curve in a comfortable softness beneath the layers of muslin. Thick, greying hair fell in a plait over her shoulder, placing her somewhere between parent and grandmother age in my mind.

"Call me Mother," she told me.

That was sure as hell not going to happen. I settled for silence instead.

Dad clutched her hands like she was saving him from drowning. "We're so happy to be here, Mother. So happy. Right, Finn? He's happy too."

I tuned out Dad's gushing and followed "Mother" into her office – if you could call it that. An empty expanse of hessian floor mats stretched out in front of us, no tables or chairs. Mother knelt down in the middle of it, folding her hands expectantly. I glanced at Dad. I doubted he'd be able to get up again if he sat on the floor, and that was if he made it down to the mat in the first place. But there he was, folding himself into a cross-legged position, knees creaking audibly.

Mother looked at me, and I gave a shrug.

"Sure, why not?" I said under my breath. I settled on the floor beside Dad.

Mother smiled and made an "mmm" sound that reminded me of the serene sigh in retreeeat. "Welcome, David. Welcome,

Finn," she said solemnly. "We normally don't invite new members at this time of year..."

I felt a surge of hope at that, but Dad's manic smile became fixed, and panic swarmed behind his eyes.

"... but we've made an exception for you and Finn." She pressed her hand to her chest, in an approximation of where her heart was. "Your story so touched us."

I had a feeling that when she said "we" or "us" it really meant her. The whole place reminded me of cloned ants rushing around after their queen. Or mother, as it was.

"I want you both to know I am here for you. We all are."

I did my best to sit patiently through her version of the "my door is always open" speech, but my ears roared with the sound of the road, and the room seemed to shift around me like the bumping of the car. If only we were still driving. If only we'd made a U-turn and sent the speedometer needle shooting straight to red as we raced back home.

Mother stood, her legs unbending and sending her body telescoping upwards in a way that didn't seem like it should be possible. My father shot up from the floor too, not telescoping like Mother, but far more agile than I'd given him credit for. I blinked, letting go of my daydreams of home. I wasn't going to be getting out of here any time soon, at least not with Dad at the wheel.

I dragged myself up. My feet had gone numb, and I stumbled against Dad in an effort to stay upright. Mother took my hand, holding it between both of hers. My palm began to sweat, even sandwiched between her chilly fingers.

"We will keep you safe here," she said, her eyes too intense – too wide and unblinking.

"Thanks, I guess." I pulled my hand away.

She looked at Dad, and her eyelids finally fluttered into a blink. "You know, I lost a child myself... a long time ago."

I swallowed, and the saliva stuck in my throat. "I'm sorry," I croaked out. And I was. I felt like an ass – Unsympathetic Douche strikes again.

"It was a car accident, also." There was a catch in her voice, and I felt my own throat tighten. "It's almost like our lives have mirrored each other's," she said. "Our accidents two halves of a whole."

She turned towards me, and her eyes were dry, absent of the tears she was pretending to swallow. Instead, they held a glazed shininess that somehow matched her serene smile. "It has been a rough path," she said, her voice no longer cracking. "But I'm so glad you have made it home to me safely."

Home? I frowned before I could stop myself. I turned to Dad, but he didn't say anything. His face had taken on that frozen look he got whenever anyone mentioned Mum and Joey. *Not here, Dad*, I said inside my head. *Not now*. I couldn't deal with Mother alone if he checked out again.

I stepped towards him, letting my forearm rest against his. There was a moment of nothing, then I felt his weight shift, leaning away from me. He was already gone, disappearing inside himself.

"Come," Mother said. "Angelina will find you some clothes."

I had a horrible feeling I knew what that meant. A woman appeared, as if summoned by the quiet mention of her name, and Mother handed us off to her. Angelina led us down a corridor; there was no macramé lining this one. My gaze dropped to

Angelina's feet and stayed there, mesmerised by the swish-glide, swish-glide of her steps. She didn't move like a normal person – too smooth and unnaturally calm. It was like a visual representation of the serene sigh in Retreat.

"You may change in here," she said, gesturing to a small, white side room. She opened a chest of drawers in the room – also white – and pulled out two bundles of muslin. "We will gather to greet you when you are ready."

Her voice was worse than her steps, melodious and so floaty she had to be high. Dad grabbed his pile of fabric, eagerly disappearing into the room. I took mine less eagerly. The fabric had very few seams, closer to bed sheets than clothes. Mine was a pale blue, and Dad's a sickly yellow colour. At least I'd be able to pick him out of the crowd.

"Dad, seriously, what the hell?" I whispered, once Angelina had shut the door behind her. "What is this place?"

"Isn't it wonderful?" Dad undressed and began looping swathes of vomit-yellow fabric around himself.

"It's ridiculous! You can't expect me to wear this." Honestly, my blue-bed-sheet outfit was the least of my concerns, but I waved it at Dad anyway.

"It's for sun protection, son. Didn't you read the information I gave you?"

I stared at him. I had read the information he'd given me all right – cover to cover, desperately looking for something which would get me out of this. Nothing had come to light.

Dad's face brightened. "If you're not sure how to put it on, I'm sure Angelina could help you." He reached for the doorknob, but I stepped in front of him.

"Dad…" I stared at him, but his eyes flicked away from mine. Like they always did.

"Fine," I said. "I'll get dressed." I unfolded the bundle of fabric.

"And change your shoes." Dad nodded to a pair of soft, slipper-like moccasins on the floor by the door.

When I hesitated, Dad started another lecture. "Mother says that societies where more people wear high heels—"

"I know, I know, higher rates of depression." I'd read the study in Mother's literature. I'd read it and almost laughed that Dad was taking such a flimsy study as proof of anything. Old Dad would have been having conniptions yelling "Correlation does not equal causation!"

I kicked off my shoes. "But these aren't high heels."

I did not want to give up my sneakers, but suddenly, it seemed easier not to fight. I pulled on the slippers.

We looked like two misshapen marshmallows by the time Angelina returned. She made a pleased "mmm" sound, then gestured back towards the entrance. "Come. Everyone is waiting to welcome you."

I stared at her feet again, as we walked down the corridor. Swish-glide, swish-glide, swish-glide. Even the rhythm couldn't calm me. A pulse started up behind my eyes, and my throat tightened.

Angelina opened the door, and a line of muslin-wrapped bodies greeted us. She wasn't kidding about everyone coming out to meet us. There had to be well over a hundred adults and teenagers lined up in front of me, not to mention the group of children gathered behind them. Seeing the kids made my stomach twist even further. Who would bring their child here?

"Welcome, David. Welcome, Finn," Mother said.

"Welcome, David," the group chanted. "Welcome, Finn."

I stared at Dad, imploring him to see just how fricken weird this whole thing was, but his manic grin had turned to misty eyes, and I wasn't sure he even cared I was there anymore.

Angelina drew him forward, placing him in front of the first muslin-clad stranger. An ambiguously-pitched voice rang out from between the folds of fabric. "We will keep you safe," they said, pressing Dad's hand between both of theirs.

"Thank you," Dad whispered. Tears rolled down his cheeks. "Thank you."

And then he was being passed down the line, each figure in front of him pressing his hands between theirs. "We will keep you safe," they bleated. "We will keep you safe."

Angelina took my shoulder. "Come, Finn."

I resisted, but she pushed me towards the first set of clutching palms, and I found my hand sandwiched between them.

"We will keep you safe."

And then I was off down the line too, each sheep-person bleating the required line, then passing me to the next. The kids were playing a game, and their laughter rang out in a surreal backing track.

The line was still going. I kept my eyes on their feet and took to alternating the words "yeah" and "thanks" in response to their bleats.

"I..." a girl's voice said.

My head shot up. The word was half cut off – barely a stutter before it shut down – but it was the first thing anyone in this line had said, outside of the repeated mantra.

A pair of intense dark brown eyes met mine through the folds of fabric in front of me. Urgency lit them.

"Did you just—"

"We will keep you safe." She frowned as she spoke the line, then she squeezed my hand.

Before I could respond, she was gone, replaced by another muslin-wrapped sheep. "We will keep you safe."

I reached the end of the line and folded my arms. My hands were clammy, tingling after so much unwanted physical contact. "Dad, I can't do this. Please..."

He wasn't listening. Angelina rubbed his shoulder, as he wiped his face, tears still falling freely.

"Come," Angelina said, gesturing for me to join them. I was getting pretty sick of hearing that word from her. I wasn't some trained animal she could bark commands at, even if the bark did sound in that lilting tone.

"I'll show you to your rooms," she said. "You must rest."

Dad immediately turned, good obedient little cultist. I hesitated, then trailed after them, no other options presenting themselves. I wrapped my arms tighter around myself, scared the loosely draped clothes would slip from my shoulders. The last thing I needed right now was a display of public nudity.

Something crackled under my wrist. I glanced around. No one was watching me. I dug into my sleeve – if you could call the fabric folds that – and my fingers met a scrap of paper. I pulled it out, unfolding it.

Please take care of them, it said.

I looked back at the line of people I'd just greeted. No doubt, one of them had slipped it to me – an incantation of sorts, a continuation of the promises to keep us safe.

I shook my head. How would I survive here with all this bullshit? I screwed up the piece of paper and dropped it on the ground.

Chapter Two

"This will be your room, Finn." Angelina unlocked the door in front of us, and the lights inside turned on automatically.

We were outside a low block of prefab buildings, which ran alongside the giant fence. The rooms were tiny and peak-roofed, reminding me of a row of boatsheds.

Angelina gestured for me to go inside. "You'll stay here during your acclimation period, then you'll join the others your age in the shared dormitory."

This was certainly better than a dormitory, but I felt like I was walking into a prison cell. The lock on the outside of the door didn't fit with the peaceful-but-creepy, free-love vibes I'd been getting from the place up until now. Then again, neither did the giant fence.

"David, you'll be in one of our other blocks."

My stomach lurched. "Wait, Dad and I aren't staying together?"

Angelina shook her head. "It would be best if you spend some time apart. You have different journeys to take here."

Two weeks ago, I would have jumped at the chance for a break from Dad. Now, I wanted to cling to him.

He turned to me, actually looking me in the eye for once. Tears I didn't want to shed tightened my throat. "I love you, Dad." I wanted to say more – to plead with him as I'd been doing all day. Hell, I'd been begging him all week not to do this. But suddenly telling him I loved him seemed more important.

He nodded, then looked away. A familiar gurgling sound told me he was crying.

Angelina smiled, her face genuinely sympathetic for once, rather than that vague, floaty expression she'd worn thus far. "I will take care of him, Finn," she said. "You can rest. You've had a long journey."

It felt weirdly good to have someone acknowledge that. I just wished it was coming from someone – anyone – other than her. Why couldn't he have got help before we reached this point?

She placed a hand on my father's shoulder, gently guiding him away. I gripped the door, my fingers biting into the wood as I resisted running after him. I forced myself to look into the room, not really taking in anything except the bed.

"Dinner is at seven," Angelina called over her shoulder, back to the melodious lilting voice. "You'll hear the music, but I will come to take you to the dining hall. Until then, rest."

A heaviness came over me, as if responding to her command. I took one last look at Dad, then tore my gaze away. I crossed the threshold into my new room. It felt like a relief and a betrayal all at once. I shut the door and leaned against it, bracing for the sound of the lock clicking. It didn't come.

I lay down on the bed. There were no pillows. There was something in Mother's literature about that, some perceived risk in sleeping comfortably, like that was the biggest threat we'd ever face. Evidently, blankets didn't pose the same danger, but I didn't bother untucking the bedding. My shapeless clothes were cover enough.

I closed my eyes, waves of something washing over me. I couldn't quite call it emotion – too formless for that. But waves of sensation, weight piling down on me as it all became real. I didn't want to be here, of course I didn't. But the fact that someone else was keeping an eye on Dad – yes, that someone else would keep him "safe" – made something uncurl inside me. I felt like I could breathe for the first time in weeks.

A HIGH-PITCHED, REPEATING noise drew me awake. It would sound a few times, then stop. I found myself holding my breath, waiting for it to start again. Waiting... waiting...

I opened my eyes as I realised what it was. A cat's mew.

My first thought was that Schrödinger's cat had climbed out of Dad's lame metaphor and was hiding under my bed. Of course, if the cat meowed, there'd be no question over its mortality-status.

My second thought, as the room swirled into focus around me, was that while I was lying on a bed, it was definitely not *my* bed.

The Retreat.

I let out a long breath, covering my face.

Another mew sounded, and I peeled my hands back from my face. Was this the dinner music Angelina had told me about? I wouldn't put it past this place to play some weird-ass cat's meow music, then sit around talking about how meaningful it all was.

But no, this definitely sounded like an actual cat.

I knew from Dad's lecture that The Retreat was not down with domestic animals, so the sound of a cat – a very much alive cat – was not something I should be hearing. But as the mewing continued, I couldn't deny that it was coming from somewhere very close by. This room, in fact.

The thing people sometimes forget about Schrödinger's cat is that the cat is definitely alive at the start. It's trapped in a box, with poison and some radioactive junk, just so we can think very hard and feel clever about it being both alive and dead at the same time. I know it's just a thought experiment, but it's a *sick* thought experiment.

Something about that niggled at me. If the cat was in the room with me, then this was the box. The radioactive poison box.

Zombie-Finn.

That was enough to get me up and out of the bed.

I hadn't paid much attention to the furnishings earlier, frustration and exhaustion taking up all of my brain power. The roof rose in a wooden V above me, below it a solitary window, covered by a pale blind. I knew the creamy-coloured walls on either side of me connected to other rooms – probably identical to this one, but for now I could pretend I was alone. This space felt safe when I couldn't see the giant fences or swarms of people outside.

I'd only had eyes for the bed earlier, but now I stared at a wardrobe in the corner of the room. The hulking, dark wooden frame of it stared back, questioning how I could have ignored it.

Another plaintive mew sounded, confirming my suspicions. I fumbled with the old metal latch on the front of the wardrobe, until I heard a click, and the door opened a crack. Perhaps Schrödinger's wasn't the box I should have been worrying about. Was I about to unlock Pandora's pithos and release all the evils that came with it?

Dark shadows filled the inside of the wardrobe. I forced myself to feel around in there, part of me waiting for a monster's teeth to come down on my fingers. Instead, I felt the edge of a cardboard box. Inside, tiny balls of fur nudged against my hand. They squeaked at me, very much alive.

Please take care of them.

I drew my hand out, and pulled the wardrobe door open properly, revealing that there was indeed a cardboard box full of kittens inside. Who had left them in here, and why? Was it the same person who slipped me that note? I thought of the girl with the dark brown eyes. There had been so many hands – lines of strangers pressing their palms to mine, yet she was the only one who had made an impression.

A long high-pitched flute note sounded, and I spun around. *This* must be the dinner music. My eyes flew back to the kittens. I couldn't let Angelina see them.

I bundled the edge of the cardboard box closed, shutting the wardrobe door after it. The kittens' squeaking mews followed me, indignant at being confined to the dark once again.

"Shush, now, okay?" I felt like an asshole, shutting them up like that, but I was pretty sure I'd feel a whole lot worse if they were discovered. "Please?"

Maybe they understood because their cries petered out.

A knock sounded, and I took a giant step backwards away from the wardrobe. I sat down on the bed, doing my best to look like I'd been there all along.

Angelina opened the door. "Good, you're awake." She didn't apologise for bursting in uninvited, and her eyes traced around the room unashamed. It seemed I needn't have worried about the locks on the outside of the door – clearly privacy was going to be a much bigger issue than them trapping me inside.

"I need to get my bags from Mother's office," I told her.

She shook her head. "Your personal possessions will be brought to you this evening after we've finished sorting them."

Sorting them? My stuff didn't need sorting, nor did it need nosy sticky beaks poking their way through it. Angelina finally turned to me, smiling, then her expression wavered as she cast an eye up and down me. I glanced down at my robes; the fabric had rearranged itself as I slept.

"No matter. I'll help you fix it before dinner." She reached out, and I reeled back, the corner of the bed shunting under my sudden shift in weight.

The kittens mewed again at the noise. I coughed, hoping to cover the sound. "It's fine," I said loudly. "I can do it myself."

Angelina froze, her hands still reaching out, then she drew them back in, clasping her palms loosely in front of her in a way that reminded me of Mother. "All right then. Follow me when you're ready."

THE DINING HALL WAS a strange mix of family living room, school cafeteria and Retreat weirdness. Big wooden tables stood in the centre of the room, each hosting a dozen or so of The Retreat's residents. Sounds okay, apart from the fact that the tables stood only a foot or so off the ground, and the diners were sitting or kneeling on cushions.

I guess it wasn't *that* weird – people ate like this in Japan all the time – but given the obsession with safety, the tables were likely close to the ground because Mother didn't want to risk us falling off chairs.

The diners had dropped the loops of fabric from around their heads now they were indoors, and one of the knots in my stomach eased at being able to make out faces. Only one of the knots, though.

I looked for green muslin – for a pair of dark eyes staring out above it – but there were too many people in similar pastel colours, their faces blurring together.

"Is this everyone?" I asked Angelina. I scanned the room for my father. "Where's Dad?"

"Not everyone – we eat in groups, tending for each other."

Something else about the roomful of people struck me as odd. What was I saying? *Everything* about this group of people struck me as odd, but something I couldn't quite put my finger on niggled at me.

"Where are all the young people?" I asked finally. Not one of the people in front of me was under the age of twenty-five.

Angelina tilted her head a little, her smile quirking into something wry.

"I'm sorry," I rushed to add. "I didn't mean to say you're old. It's just…" I stared out at the crowd. Was I the only teenager here? That couldn't be right. Where were the children I'd seen earlier?

Angelina chuckled, and for a moment, she almost seemed like a human being, rather than the blissed-out robot she'd been up until now. "You'll be limited in who you're allowed to talk to until you've acclimated. We need to keep everyone safe."

Was I in some kind of quarantine? Angelina took my arm, guiding me towards a table at the front of the room. "You'll sit over here with me and Mother this week," she said.

I pulled away from her. "But where's my dad?"

Angelina smiled, unphased by my persistence. "Adults follow a different path when they first arrive. He'll be eating separately." She reached for my arm again.

I stepped back. "Then I'll wait – I'll eat with him. I want to see my dad." Guilt gnawed at my stomach. I shouldn't have let them take him away. I shouldn't have been relieved to have some time alone.

Angelina's lips tightened. She opened her mouth to speak, but Mother appeared beside me. I jumped, my heart giving a squeeze at her sudden presence.

"Peace, Finn." She pressed her hand to my chest, palm against my sternum. "We're all family here, you don't need to fear being alone."

I flinched, tensing, ready to shove her away. The warmth of her fingers crept through the muslin wrap to my skin, halting me. My pulse echoed back, pounding against my rib cage. I felt it slow, not-quite-calm settling over me, as if her hand held a hypnotic power.

"There was a girl," I told her, god knows why. "Earlier, in the line. Is she here?" I knew she wasn't – she must have been around my age, and was therefore being kept away from me. My voice sounded strained, an edge of pleading creeping in.

"Maybe." Mother studied me, her expression gentle. Of course she wouldn't know who I meant just from "there was a girl". I strained the recesses of my memory for identifying features. There was nothing except those dark eyes. Mother tapped her palm on my chest, mimicking my heartbeat.

I stared back at her. This was weird as all hell – far too intimate and close from a stranger – and yet I hadn't pulled away. Something inside me wanted to lean against her round shoulders and let her hug me, let her comfort me like her title promised.

Mother stroked my hair back and smiled, as if she understood all the thoughts running through my head. "Come sit beside me, Finn. You're safe here."

I nodded, and I sat. Warmth radiated from her presence, and I took a long breath, feeling it shudder just a little. Someone placed a plate in front of me and I stared at it. I was shutting down. This day had been too much, too long, too intense.

"Eat," Mother prompted, gently, and I ate, spooning food into my mouth without tasting it.

This made her smile stretch. "Good boy."

The food stuck in my throat, and I coughed. Mother patted my hand, soothing me or just cutting me off, I wasn't sure. She wasn't my mother; my mother was gone. And with every minute they kept me from him, I wondered if my dad was too.

DINNER DRAGGED ON, with conversations and laughter flowing around me. My knee started to jiggle, and I pressed it down firmly with my hand. If only my anxiety was that easy to squash.

"Can I go back to my room?" I asked Mother.

She rested her hand on top of mine, keeping me in place. "Not yet. Mealtime conversation is food for the soul. Health of the soul feeds health of the body."

This was further down the woo-woo scale than I was comfortable with. What would be best for my soul would be to get back to my room and check on the kittens. Visions of opening the box and finding them all dead floated through my mind – starved, dehydrated and neglected by me. I shuddered at the image.

Finally, Mother stood, everyone else rising with her. I stumbled up, my feet numb with pins and needles once again. Mother and Angelina each caught one of my hands, trapping me there.

"Together we breathe; together we are safe," Mother said.

"Together we breathe; together we are safe," everyone except me intoned back. They all took a deep, synchronised breath, letting it out with a gentle "ahh" sound. Mother's grip softened, and I pulled my hands free, crossing them tightly over my stomach. Definitely too much woo.

She turned to me. "You may now return to your room, Finn. Angelina will show you the way." She glanced at Angelina. "Walk safely, both of you."

Angelina linked her arm through mine, perhaps worried I'd run away if left unattended. I couldn't say she was completely off base; running had occurred to me.

"Hood up," Angelina said as we stepped outside. She took one end of the fabric looped around my shoulders and placed it over my head.

"I thought it was for sun protection." I glanced at the darkening sky, then back at Angelina.

"There are many dangers in the atmosphere," she said solemnly.

"I think I'll risk it." I pulled the fabric back to my shoulders, daring her to challenge me. Angelina just pursed her lips.

She walked me back across the grounds. I scanned the people we passed, hoping for glimpses of faces between the folds of fabric. Nothing familiar greeted me – no sign of Dad's beard or the girl's dark eyes. They were all shapeless clones.

Angelina opened my door for me. "Tomorrow, you may explore the grounds, but tonight you must stay here, understand?"

I nodded. I understood, all right. I couldn't guarantee I was going to obey. I stepped inside, then turned around and leaned my hands on either side of the doorframe, barring the entry with my body.

"Lights out is at ten p.m. You must sleep then." Angelina smiled at me, her expression expectant, though whether for questions or arguments, I wasn't sure. When I didn't respond, she continued. "You are free to do what you wish – inside your room – until the lights go out."

"Goodnight, then." I started to shut the door.

"Sleep safely," she called before the latch clicked into place.

I watched through the window until she'd crossed the grounds. Normally I would have told her to take a hike if she thought I was going to sit in my room alone for however long it was until 10pm, but I had something more important to think about. I made a beeline for the wardrobe. Plaintive mews rose up, my movement waking them. The box of kittens was still there, very much not a figment of my imagination.

"Please take care of them" was all well and good, but it didn't exactly give me instructions on how. The Retreat was completely vegetarian. I'd just chowed my way through an entire meal without giving much thought to the difference, but I had a feeling I'd have some trouble convincing a box of kittens to eat lentils.

I bent the wardrobe door right back, letting in the light. The box was lined with straw, which seemed to be going some way towards absorbing the smell of cat piss. Fortunately, none of them had crapped themselves yet.

A jug of milk sat in a bowl of ice and water on a small shelf right at the back, above the box. I could have sworn it hadn't been there earlier... which meant someone had been in my room.

I glanced around, as if I would find them crouched in a corner. Of course no one was there. Whoever this was, they were smart enough not to stick around long enough to get caught.

At the bottom of the wardrobe there were a couple of extra boxes packed full of clean, dry straw. I had a feeling that was going to come in handy very soon.

I lifted one of the kittens onto my lap. There was a plate under the bowl of water, and I slipped it out, pouring some of the milk onto it.

"Come on, little fluffball," I said, holding the kitten up to the plate of milk. "I know it's not quite a saucer, but you can still lap this up, right?"

The kitten wriggled and squirmed, and the others in the box mewed, squeaking louder at the separation. "See, your brothers and sisters want some milk. Come on, drink."

The kitten stretched out its paws, tiny claws splayed. An eyedropper would have made this much simpler. My mum had been a vet, so I'd done my share of helping feed baby animals in the past. I'd even thought about studying veterinary science myself, until the day a dog came in after eating half a block of chocolate and I realised just how much vomit mum dealt with on a daily basis. Not to mention the blood. Turns out I'm an absolute sook about bodily fluids.

Had Mum and I fed kittens with cow's milk? I couldn't remember if they could drink that. I sniffed the jug. *Was* this even cow's milk? It smelt different to the homogenised supermarket milk – richer – and it had separated, a foamy cream crust coating the surface. Honestly, the whole thing grossed me out, but I wasn't exactly spoilt for options of what to feed them otherwise.

I dipped my hand into the jug, dripping milk from my fingers into the kitten's mouth. Its tongue moved, licking at the liquid.

"See, that's not so bad, is it?"

The kitten licked my finger, clearly agreeing. I repeated the process a few times, dipping my hand into the jug and letting the milk drip. The kitten happily licked it up. "All right, little fluffball. Let's let your brothers and sisters have some." I gently placed the kitten back in the box, picking out the next one. "Come on, Fluffball Two. Hopefully you'll get the hang of this as quickly as your sibling did."

I did a quick count. Eight kittens. At this rate, feeding them might take me all the way up to lights out – not that I was planning on honouring their stupid rules. Kittens slept most of the time, right? Hopefully they'd stay quiet in the box tomorrow and not draw attention to themselves. Or to me.

I picked up the next kitten, giving them their share of the milk. I needed to find the girl with the dark eyes. I could feed the kittens milk for now, but eventually they were going to need meat, and I wasn't planning on catching and butchering mice. At what age were cats self-sufficient? Perhaps I could release them under the fence and let them fend for themselves? Even fighting for survival had to be better than living their whole lives in a box.

I put the kitten down, ignoring the squeaking pleas from the ones yet to be fed. Why was I sitting here guessing when a quick Google search would tell me everything I needed to know? I reached for my pocket automatically, but of course the shapeless robes didn't have any.

I glanced around. My bag sat on the end of the bed, brought to my room, as promised... but it didn't look right. The top curved down, innards deflated.

"No, no, no..."

The zip had been straining when I left home. Dad said I could only take one bag with me, so I'd packed it to bursting with every memory I could cram in there.

The kittens whimpered as if in response to my distress. I yanked what remained out of the bag, tossing it onto the floor. My clothes were gone – my favourite jeans and hoodie, gone.

I tore the shapeless blue garment off, hurling it at the pile of clothes. "Fucking cult!"

T-shirts and boxers – that's all they'd left me. Stuff I could wear under their stupid muslin wraps.

Squeaks from the wardrobe rose up in protest at my outburst.

"Fucking kittens!"

I couldn't be responsible for them. I had to get out of this bloody place.

A grinding clunk sounded, startling me out of my tantrum. I froze, and even the kittens momentarily quietened at the noise. Everything stilled for a second. Then a second clunk, and everything went black.

"What the…?"

Something one step up from fear clutched at my throat. I fumbled my way across the room, tripping over the pile of clothes I'd just thrown on the floor. When I say everything went black, I mean *black*. We were so far away from the road or any other traces of civilisation, that the darkness was absolute. I'd never been afraid at night-time, but maybe that was because I'd never before experienced true, solid darkness.

I kept moving, scrambling over to the bed. I fumbled around until I found my bag set on top of it. Dad had told me personal electronics weren't allowed at The Retreat. He'd waited until an hour before we left, perhaps scared I'd chuck a wobbly if I'd had more time to think about it. As it happens, an hour is plenty of time to cut a slit in the lining of your bag and stash your phone inside.

I felt around at the bottom, locating the edge of the torn fabric but nothing else. No familiar hard rectangle, no source of light. Someone – probably Mother – had found the phone and removed it.

I sank down on the edge of the bed, closing my eyes. Not that it made any difference. Solid black greeted me, eyes open or closed. I got up, and ran a hand over the wall, searching for a switch. To hell with their lights-out rule.

The switch should have been by the door, right? That was the logical place if you weren't intentionally trying to screw with people.

No cool plastic bump appeared under my fingertips. I swept them back and forth over the wall, growing more frantic with each pass. A sickening realisation came over me. There was no switch. The dark was so utterly solidly black because none of these pastel-draped sheep-people had control of their own light.

That one-step-up-from-fear feeling built in my throat again. I wanted to scream, to kick or punch something, but there was nothing to hit. I lashed out at the darkness anyway. My hand connected with a solid object, and pain shot up my arm. I let out a shout, clutching my closed fist to my chest.

The mewing stopped, the sudden silence absolute.

"Fuck," I whispered.

A flood of guilt washed the sharp shards of anger from me. I hadn't meant to scare the poor sorry kittens. It wasn't their stupid fault they were stuck in my cupboard with only me to feed them.

I eased my fingers in and out of a clench. The movement was painful, but not impossible. Not broken. That was one positive for this miserable day.

Now that I'd taken a moment to breathe, the room was not the solid inky black it had been when the lights first went out. The sky outside the window was a dirty grey.

"Morning is coming," I told myself. It would get darker before it got lighter, but morning would come eventually. I could hold out until morning.

Another breath, and I could see outlines of the room – nothing clearly, no detail, just silhouettes as my eyes adjusted. It was the wardrobe that my hand had connected with. No wonder the kittens were scared.

I felt my way over to it, then reached into the box. There were still two kittens to be fed. I had no way of knowing which were which, but I just had to hope that if I kept dripping milk into their mouths, eventually all of them would get their share.

I sat down in the dark and dipped my fingers into the jug of milk. I wrinkled my nose. The texture of the creamy crust bothered me more now I could only feel rather than see the slime of it. Still. The kittens had to eat.

Think of something calming, Finn, I told myself. *You have to stay calm.*

The moment I thought that, I started to panic again. Calm. Calm. It was like I'd forgotten how to breathe.

In and out, Finn, said a familiar voice inside my head. *How is that so hard?*

I half smiled. That's exactly how Carly would say it. Pissed off by my panicking, but still willing to help me through it.

Carly. My neighbour. Carla Theroux to everyone else – Carly-Throw to me. I felt my heartrate slow as I thought about her. Carly could keep me calm. She was about the only person that ever could. God, I missed her.

I picked up another kitten, trying not to let my thoughts stray as I did. Something dripped off my chin, and I realised I was crying. But I couldn't give into it. I had to stay calm.

I stared at the window, at the weak light coming through it. At home, Carly's bedroom window was opposite mine.

That's right, keep focusing on me, you weirdo, Carly's voice in my head told me. *That'll stop you crying.*

Every night I'd watch her bedside light flick on and off. On – she'd thought of an idea. Off – she'd finished writing it down. On – her pen was scratching its way across her yellow-paged notebook again. She always had dark circles under her eyes from staying up half the night writing. So did I from being woken up every time.

That light flicking on and off all night used to drive me nuts, but I'd have given anything to see it now, instead of sitting in Mother's enforced darkness.

I picked up the next kitten, clutching it to my chest as it mewed desperately for food. I tucked its warm body under my chin, not caring that I was probably soaking it in tears.

Carly never once let me read what was in her notebooks. She said she only would if I kept one too. Turns out, I'm not the type of guy that has notebook-worthy ideas.

"It's all right, little dude," I told the kitten. "I'm going to look after you." That wasn't enough of a promise. The kitten was so light – so helpless. My stomach clenched at the idea of something so tiny being entirely dependent on me. But I felt something else growing inside me. Resolve. I needed to get home – back to Carly, and back to my real life. And these kittens needed me to help them.

Whatever it took, I was going to get us all out of here.

Chapter Three

*W*ebs of cracks spread across the glass in front of me. The seatbelt cut into my neck, pinning me against the head-rest. I turned, stretching out for Joey's hand. I couldn't reach it. A single trickle of blood ran down her fingers, over the edge of her booster seat, onto the upholstery. She shrieked, a high repeating scream that cut through me.

Mum's breathing was fast. Too fast. Too shallow.

I turned to her. Her face was pale, and her eyes wide. "You have to get out. Go get help, Finn. You have to get out."

I STARTED AWAKE AT the sound of a scream.

Carly's pixie-cut-framed face still swam in front of me, and I looked automatically to the right, searching for the window, expecting to see her house through it. Instead, I saw only the blank wall of my bare room at The Retreat.

It must have been the early hours of the morning, based on the weak light creeping in around the blind of the real window. Light – thank god. Morning was coming. I shuddered at the memory of the total darkness.

I was on the floor, my neck bent awkwardly against the end of the bed. One of the kittens was asleep in my lap. I peeked in at the others, relieved to see their little stomachs rising and falling in sleeping breaths. The inevitable had happened, and my nose wrinkled at the smell of their shit mixed in with the straw.

I placed the kitten carefully back in the box with its brothers and sisters, then stumbled across the room. The door's hinges creaked as I opened it and peered out.

The darkness may have given way to the grey of the dawn sky, but the creepy stillness sent shivers of fear through me. I stared out at the trees beyond the fence. So many trees stretching out and out.

And then, a flicker of movement caught my eye – a trail of muslin-hooded figures moving silently through the trees. They looked like ghosts. Malevolent spirits, drifting through the forest.

But I didn't believe in ghosts. And the idea of them being human scared me even more.

Sweat beaded on my forehead, and I began to shake. I'd been calling this place a cult, but I hadn't really believed it. All manner of awful things – rituals, human sacrifice, abuse – ran through my head now. But most of all, that scream.

I closed the door, and leaned back against it, sliding down to the floor.

Someone had screamed. Someone needed help. My mother's voice echoed in my head. *Go get help, Finn. You have to leave us. Go get help.*

But I couldn't move. I couldn't go out there. Those silent shrouded figures marched through my mind, locking me in place just as thoroughly as if they had been in the room circling me.

Once again, I was failing. Once again, someone was hurt, and I was doing nothing to save them.

I WOKE PROPERLY IN the morning, still slumped against the door. For a moment, the image of the cracked windscreen floated in front of me, the web of lines snaking across my vision as if they would wrap around and strangle me.

Don't think about it, I told myself. Not now. I made myself blink – once, twice – and finally the present world became clear.

I eased myself up, rolling my shoulders as I did. I was going to end up with some serious neck issues if I didn't start sleeping in the bed.

The kittens were all awake in the box, clambering over each other to mew plaintively for food. They stank, but we'd done it. We'd all made it through the night.

I tipped most of the straw out of one of the extra boxes, then transferred the kittens into it. Their cries grew louder, but I didn't think it was about the change of scenery. They wanted food, and everything else would be a letdown right now.

"In a minute, little dudes," I told them. "Just got to do some housekeeping."

I slipped out of my room, taking the old box with me. There must be rubbish bins somewhere. Outside the dining room? I started to cross the compound, but the sound of voices made me freeze. I had approximately zero ideas of how to explain holding a box full of straw and cat shit that didn't involve exposing the kittens.

I scanned the yard, looking for anywhere to stash it. A wooden compost bin on the other side of the vegetable patch caught my eye. Probably not exactly hygienic to chuck cat waste in there, but it would have to do.

I dashed over and lifted the bin lid. An earthy smell, a mix of rotting food and mould, floated out. At least it would disguise the cat scent. I tipped the soiled straw in, then turned the compost a couple of times with a trowel to disguise it. Heat rose up as I did, hitting my face uncomfortably. The whole thing reeked.

"You owe me, little fluffballs," I muttered.

I booked it back to my room, only letting myself relax once the door was closed. I leaned against it and closed my eyes, my breaths coming heavy and hard. Who would have thought I'd have this much excitement on my first day in a cult?

The kittens' mews had reached a new peak volume. I opened the wardrobe door. "Don't worry, little fluffballs. I haven't forgotten you."

I fed them, moving quickly now I'd got the hang of it. Not fast enough for them, by the sound of their cries, but slowly they quieted down, as each one got their fill. The level of the jug had gone down more than I would have liked from only two feeds. What would I do when the milk ran out?

A soft knock sounded at the door just as I was finishing up with the last one. Jeez, even the door knocks came out sounding like serene sighs here. I bundled the kitten back into its box and closed the wardrobe.

"Is that you, Dad?" I called.

There was a pause, then the door opened and Mother walked in. I stood and took a massive step forward, trying to put as much distance as possible between us and the wardrobe.

"Hi," I said, a little too loudly. Hopefully the sound of my heart pounding would mask any noise the kittens made. If Mother noticed the lingering smell of cat excrement or sour milk, she had the grace not to mention it.

"Good morning, Finn," she said. "I trust you slept safely."

I nodded dumbly. How does one sleep unsafely? I'm not sure my feline companions and scrunched position on the floor were conducive to a good night's rest, but it was hardly bungee jumping.

"Actually, no," I said, remembering. "I thought I heard someone scream, and..." I cut myself off before mentioning the trail of people heading out into the trees. I wasn't supposed to have been outside to see that, and I didn't want to risk her deciding to lock my door at night to keep me inside.

A flash of something hard crossed Mother's face, then she smoothed her expression back out into her usual serene one.

"It must have been a nightmare," she said.

Yeah, but mine or someone else's?

"The power is about to come back on," she added. "It's time to head to the bathrooms to wash up." She sniffed, somehow managing to keep her face neutral.

Let her think it's me, I thought. *Let her believe I stink of sour milk and cat piss, so she'll keep her distance.*

"The power was off?" I asked. That seemed like overkill. Surely they could have just cut the lights without shutting down the whole grid.

"Electrical fires are one of the leading causes of death, especially in the early hours of the morning."

"Okay..."

What on earth else could I say to that? I'm sure electrical fires were a problem, but weren't there just as many dangers in making everything dark and cold with no power?

Mother studied my face. "Make sure you shave while you're in the bathroom."

I touched my face, the stubble scratching my palm. "I'm growing a beard," I said. I'd had approximately zero plans to grow a beard up until now, but anything to rile this woman up.

"Beards are not allowed here. They're not safe."

"Beards aren't safe?" I stared at her, unable to hide my utter bafflement at her words.

"You may read the studies after your acclimation period if you wish." Mother's voice was final, no room for discussion.

Sure. I'd love to read a "study" that told me beards "weren't safe". What a load of croc. I bet Dad was loving this bit. I'd never seen him anything close to clean shaven.

"Can I go talk to my dad, now?" I asked. *And tell him I want to get the hell out of here*, I added in my head.

Mother smiled, her face bland and serene. "You won't be seeing your father today," she said. "You'll be entering the silent phase of your acclimation period."

"Silent phase?"

She nodded. "Yes, we don't allow speech in the first few weeks."

I opened my mouth, but shut it again, too baffled to form a sensible answer.

She nodded and beamed at me, the smile stretching further than should be possible. "Yes, like that. Silence."

I shook my head. "What are you—?"

She pressed her finger to my lips. "Silence," she said again.

MOTHER LED ME TO THE bathrooms, ignoring my protests, and handed me off to a figure wrapped in light brown, who also ignored everything I said. I guess my "silent phase" was going to produce the equivalent of little kids sticking their fingers in their ears with a determined shout of "I can't hear you!".

After I showered – and yes, shaved – the figure handed me a new, clean bundle of fabric, pastel pink this time. That answered my questions about whether they always wore the same colours... and dashed my hopes of finding the girl with the dark eyes by looking for her in green.

I sat through another weird meal, between Mother and Angelina, then made my way back to my room. A note taped to the door told me to *Relax, Explore, Find Yourself, and Stay Safe*. The door itself was locked.

I leaned my head against it, doing my best to develop animal-psychic powers. *I'll be back to feed you as soon as I can*, I told the kittens. If they were still in there, that was. I couldn't shake the feeling the locked door might mean we'd been discovered. Then again, they had no reason to search my room. They'd taken 90 percent of my possessions, and it wasn't like I knew anyone here who could slip me contraband. What even passed for contraband here? Normal shoes?

I dragged myself away, not wanting to cast suspicion just in case. I milled around pretty much aimlessly. Find myself... what was that supposed to mean? Last time I checked, I wasn't lost. I was Finn Bryant – high school student, son of David and Noleen Bryant, brother of Joey. I swallowed. That wasn't a good place to start.

But I still wasn't lost. I was a high school student, a good athlete. Well, okay, *average* athlete might be more accurate. I made the soccer, cross country and basketball teams at my school, but I was hardly the star. I supported other people to get the goals rather than scoring them myself. That was a thing, though, wasn't it? Being the back up?

Carly was a star. She was a writer. She did a whole heap of drama and other artsy stuff too, and she was amazing at all of it. I just did sports so I was doing *something*, without really giving a crap what it was.

A horrible thought occurred to me. Did I just do team sports as a way to avoid having to have a personality of my own? Did I even have a personality?

I stumbled, tripping over my own feet. I was in the middle of the yard, with no clear memory of walking here. Suddenly the fences, which had seemed to close in around me last night, stretched out, looming above me. I felt unmoored. My breathing was coming way too fast, and I shook my head fiercely, trying to make it slow down.

Snap out of it, Finn! Carly yelled in my head.

I forced myself to take a long, slow inhale. Now was not the time for an existential crisis. Bloody cult. I'd been here less than twenty-four hours, and all it had taken was a post-it note telling me to find myself to start a breakdown.

I started walking again, trying to keep my steps and my breathing steady this time. I forced myself to stay present, taking in my surroundings. Whatever I had been back home, I wasn't that anymore. Maybe I *was* lost after all.

Muslin-clad people nodded to me as I passed them. I kept walking without returning the gesture.

It soon became clear that I could do almost whatever I wanted. Except speak, of course. Whenever I made even the slightest attempt at vocalisation, the people around me would turn away, their backs a forceful shun until I fell silent again. Don't get me wrong, they were kind in their own screwed-up way. Whenever I needed something, like food or to know where the bathrooms were, I'd find it pressed into my hands or a gentle touch on my shoulder guiding me to where I needed to be.

The only thing they didn't guide me towards was my father. "We will keep you safe," they all said. Apparently, the silence only applied to me.

I wandered over to the fence. It was made up of a wire grid, like the fences at my old school, only thicker. I curled my fingers through it, testing the tension. On the other side was a river, just begging to be swum in.

I looked around, spotting a gate. Just beyond it was another building. No one had told me what was in that one, which must mean it was important.

I glanced back at the figures behind me. No one seemed to be paying me any attention.

I walked slowly over to the gate, keeping my steps even so as not to draw attention to myself. About half a pace away from it, I saw the padlock. I felt my shoulders slump in response, but

I took hold of it anyway. To my surprise, the lock came off in my hand. I pushed the gate open and stepped through, taking a deep breath. I knew it wasn't really possible, but the air tasted sweeter on this side of the fence, easier to breathe.

A hand clamped down on my shoulder. I jumped, spinning around. A woman stood beside me. She pulled me back towards the compound.

"But I want to—"

She pressed her finger to my lips, not turning away, but not allowing me to speak either. "The fences are there to keep you safe, Finn. You mustn't stray beyond them," she said, and guided me back through the gate. It felt so odd that she knew my name without me having any inkling of hers.

She took the padlock from me, fitting it back into place, then picked up the end of my muslin wrap, which I'd let fall from my shoulders. She looped it back around my head. "The wraps protect you from the sun, you must keep them on."

Her face was warm, kindly, and speckled brown – from a lifetime of tanning rather than genetics, I suspected. I wondered if she saw the irony of forcing sun-safety on me.

I glanced back towards the building on the other side of the fence.

She placed her hand on my shoulder again, guiding me away. "It's nothing exciting, Finn. Just the kitchen. It's on the other side of the fence to reduce hazards, nothing more interesting than that." Her voice was gentle, but more solid than Angelina's. Calm, but like *actually* calm, not that weird floaty bullshit Angelina and Mother seemed to waft everywhere.

"There are reasons for everything, you will see. I know the silence is hard," she said. "But you will find value in that too, I promise."

"Okay," I told her, and then pressed my lips together, almost laughing at the fact I was agreeing to stop talking by talking.

Her eyes crinkled, clearly seeing the humour in it too. "Are you thirsty?" She led me over to a cooler outside the dining room. It was filled with jugs of water, a rack of cups beside it.

There was no milk, but something almost as good lined the bottom of the tub – ice.

I filled a glass for myself, and one for my companion, using it as an excuse to examine the set up. The glasses sat in racks, one for clean, one for dirty. It would be obvious if one were missing, so I tossed out the idea of slipping a cup of ice under my robe. I'd have to palm chunks of the stuff, sneaking them back to my room bit by bit. Once my door was unlocked, that was. The ice would burn my hands, but it wasn't like I had other options. These kittens were *really* going to owe me if I got frostbite for them.

The woman drank deeply from her glass of water, then set it down on the dirty rack.

"Thank you, Finn." She touched my shoulder one more time, gently squeezing it. I relaxed at her touch, but not in the sudden, confusing way I had last night when Mother had pressed her hand against my heart. This was just a small moment of connection. Reassurance that she was real – that I was real – still me, not one of these clones. Besides, she reminded me more of my real mother than the creepy Mother I was supposed to follow did.

She leaned forward. "Don't tell anyone you found the gate unlocked," she whispered. She turned away before I could answer, disappearing into the crowd of fabric-wrapped figures.

Interesting. Did that mean someone had been using the gate for nefarious purposes, or was she simply trying to protect whoever had made a careless mistake?

That raised another less interesting, more disturbing question: there were so many rules here – all supposedly in the name of safety – but no one had yet told me what the punishment was for breaking any of them. I had a feeling I didn't want to know.

I walked loops around the compound, the rhythm of my pacing steadying me. The rebuffs each time I tried to speak grew old, so I kept to their rule of silence. My stomach knotted every time I passed my room. I tried the door each time, but it was still locked. I listened for distressed meows and heard nothing. I wasn't sure whether that was a good or a bad thing. I didn't want them crying, feeling abandoned in the dark, but at least if they were making noise I'd know they were still there – still alive, no Schrödinger nonsense.

Bored of walking loops, I made my way around the side of the dining hall. A flat grassy area spread out in the centre of The Retreat, reminding me of the sports field at school. It wasn't closed off, I could walk in there, but buildings lined it on four sides, only footpath-sized gaps between them.

I hesitated. Here were the young people – little children all the way up to teenagers, all of them dressed in those muslin wraps. Relief and revulsion battled inside me at the sight. Seeing people my own age washed away some of the isolation I'd been feeling, but at the same time, there was something so perverse about seeing little kids trapped here, all wrapped up like shapeless clones of their parents. At least the adults had a choice.

"You shouldn't be here," a voice said.

A hand touched my shoulder, and I spun around, flinching away, still not used to so much physical contact. The owner of the hand flinched too, drawing back.

"I'm sorry," she said. "I did not mean... it's just you're not allowed near the children during your acclimation period."

I stared into the girl's wide, dark brown eyes. "You!" I said. "I've been looking everywhere for you."

The girl's lips parted, but then her gaze dropped to the ground. "You're not supposed to talk, Finn."

"But it was you, wasn't it?" I stepped in close, lowering my voice. Around us, other people turned away, shutting my un-wanted words out, but I couldn't risk them overhearing. "The note – the kittens – it was you?"

She bit her lip, then nervously glanced around. She met my eye and gave the tiniest nod.

"Turn away, Aria," Mother's voice boomed out, no pretence of calm. She strode towards us from across the grass, Angelina following after her. "Turn away now!" Mother said.

The girl – Aria – grabbed my hand, pulling me close to whisper in my ear. "Please look after them. Don't let her find them!"

"But how—"

Her hand whipped out of mine as Mother grabbed her shoulders, forcibly turning her away. Angelina grabbed my shoulders, pulling me back.

"No! Just let me talk to her." I shoved Angelina, trying to get close to Aria.

Mother held Aria's face cupped in her hands. "What did he say to you, Aria? What did he say?"

Aria shook her head. "Nothing, Mother. He told me nothing."

I charged towards her, reaching for her hand. "Aria!"

She looked up, face pale. She shook her head ever so slightly, her eyes darting towards Mother. It wasn't just about the kittens anymore. I had to talk to her; I had to! They'd taken my stuff; they'd taken my dad... I couldn't live like this if they kept taking everything away.

"Please!" I yelled. "I just want to talk to you."

My voice had become a shriek. Aria stepped back, her eyelids flickering in rapid, frightened blinks.

Two men appeared beside me, then two sets of arms closed around me. They pulled me away as Aria stared at me, making no move to stop them.

Chapter Four

I fought against the men as they forced me back towards my room. "Let me go!" I twisted, managing to break free. I sprinted back towards the kids' area, but one of the men tackled me. My head hit the ground hard. I whirled around, kicking him in the stomach. He let out a groan, and then his fist collided with my face.

"Stop!" Mother called out. "Don't hurt him!"

I blinked, dazed. My nose was bleeding, I knew that much. Then Mother's hands were cupping the sides of my jaw. She crouched beside me, peering into my eyes, and an expression I couldn't read crossed her face. I blinked again as everything went double.

She glared up at the man who had hit me. "You will not use violence here!" She hesitated for a moment, then turned to the other man. "Take him to the Repercussion Rooms."

The men's faces blanched. I wasn't sure whether to be relieved for myself or terrified for the man being sent away.

"Mother…" he said. "It was an accident. I didn't mean—"

"Take him," Mother said again, her voice final. I looked away, not wanting to know whether or not the other man complied.

"What about Finn?" Angelina asked.

Mother turned back to me. Her hands gently caressed the sides of my face for a moment, then her expression hardened. "Lock him in his room."

"No!" I tried to scramble up, but two more men appeared, almost like they really were clones. They hauled me up and marched me back to my room. In seconds, they had opened the door and thrown me in there. Actually *thrown* me. Mother's warnings about not using violence apparently meant nothing.

I landed with a thump against the side of the bed. I leapt up, racing back to the door, but a click sounded before I reached it.

Locked in. Trapped. Just like I'd feared.

I slammed my fists against the door anyway. "Let me out, you mother—" I cut myself off. Even in this state, I saw the humour in nearly calling them that. I almost wanted to yell "Pun fully intended!"

I pounded on the door, ready to tear it to shreds with my bare hands if I had to. "Let me out!" They couldn't keep me here. They couldn't trap me like this. They couldn't take everything from me.

The door didn't yield, but my nails did. They tore back at the roots on my right hand. I welcomed the blood, smearing it across the door.

I tore the sheets from the bed, getting blood on those too, then threw them to the floor. The mattress was next, then everything else I could get my hands on. I pounded on the walls, my chest heaving in heavy sobs.

It was all gone. My life. My family. Everything was gone.

I LAY IN THE MESS I'D created for a long time before I remembered the kittens. I sat up. Nausea flooded me as I looked around at the shattered room. The noise I must have made – the thumps and vibrations. I got up and opened the wardrobe door.

The kittens lay curled together in the back of the box, still breathing but silent. I'd scared them. Guilt rolled in my stomach, mixing with anger at my own stupid selfishness. It was almost enough to send me into another rage. What was wrong with me? Why did I have to behave like such an asshole?

I grabbed the jug of milk, forcing myself to calm down. They deserved someone better than me to take care of them. Someone not so broken. But until I could talk to Aria, I was all they had.

I reached into the box, gently lifting out one of the kittens. "Hey little guy, it's okay. It's okay." The kitten squirmed in my grip, calming only when I produced the milk. I fed him with my left hand, not wanting my bloody fingers to contaminate their food. "I know, buddy. I know. You lost your mum too, didn't you?"

A lump formed in my throat, and I tried not to follow that train of thought. Something awful must have happened to end up with eight kittens shoved in a box in a wardrobe, just like something awful had happened to end with me getting myself locked in this room.

You have to get out...

... Go get help, Finn.

You have to get out... Finn... Finn...

I pushed the accident from my mind, concentrating only on feeding my charges.

Slowly, they started to trust me again. By the time I placed the third one back in the box, they were making small mewing sounds, eagerly crawling towards me for their turn.

"It's okay, little dudes. I've got you."

I was starting to be able to tell them apart – their personalities and faces taking shape in my mind. The one with the orange spot that looked like a moustache was always first to be fed, not because he was the keenest, but because he was the slowest at squirming away from my hand when I reached in to pick them up. I didn't know whether the kitten was a boy or a girl, of course, but I'd found myself assigning genders to them unintentionally. The one with the shortest tail was a girl, I'd decided. She liked to stretch out with her tiny claws, perhaps to compensate for her shortcomings. The one with a hint of tabby stripes often chewed on my thumb, already craving meat.

"You need names, don't you, little dudes?"

I frowned, cutting that idea short. No. I couldn't name them. I couldn't keep them. And I wouldn't be able to hide them for much longer. The hopelessness of both our situations settled over me. "We'll be okay, little dudes. I'll figure something out."

I placed the last kitten back in the box. Truthfully, all I really wanted right now was to curl up and sleep, but I'd destroyed the bed. I could have put the mattress back on the base – picked up the sheets and remade everything. Somehow, it didn't feel honest to do that. I had created this mess, and now I had to own it. Besides, a part of me wanted the people from

The Retreat – Mother – to see what I had done. To see what I was capable of. Surely they would expel us if they knew how damaged Dad and I really were?

I lay down in the pile of bedding. The floor was what I deserved, after all.

A LIGHT KNOCK ON THE door and the sound of a key turning in the lock woke me later. I opened my eyes but didn't move. Before we got here, I never used to sleep during the day. Now it was all I wanted to do.

The door opened, but only part way, the bundled-up sheet wedging against it. I could have pulled it free, but I wasn't going to help these people any more than I had to.

"Finn?" a soft voice called out.

I sat up. It sounded like the woman who had stopped me going through the gate.

She pushed on the door again, opening it just enough to squeeze inside. Her eyes took in the room – the destroyed bed, the blood-smears on the door, and of course me, lying in the middle of it like the utter piece of crap I was. Her expression didn't change; no anger or judgement filled her face, just a slight frown. She seemed more concerned than anything else.

She let the quiet hang for a moment, simply breathing with me. Normally, it would have creeped me out, but somehow from her, the silence was calming.

"May I sit?" she said finally.

I nodded. It was nice to have someone here actually ask permission for something, instead of constantly telling me what to do. She folded herself up, sitting cross legged at the edge of the blankets. "I didn't introduce myself before. My name's Anabelle. Mother asked me to come sit with you."

"I'm sorry," I whispered. And I was. I didn't want to be here, but that wasn't these people's fault. I didn't have the right to destroy their stuff just because I was angry at Mother and my dad.

The woman nodded. She didn't tell me not to speak, so I guess this was a reprieve from my enforced period of silence.

"I understand," she said. "I was very angry when I arrived here. Most of us were."

I couldn't picture it – the floaty clones I'd seen drifting around the compound didn't look like they had the capacity for mild irritation, let alone full-out anger. Certainly, none of them seemed capable of the rage I seemed to have inside me. Well, except for the man who had hit me, but I couldn't exactly claim that was unprovoked.

"This isn't the first time you've lost control, is it?" Annabelle asked.

I wasn't sure whether she was really asking. Dad would have told them about the fights I'd got into since Mum and Joey died – the way I'd trashed my room because I'd found one of Joey's drawings in my desk. I couldn't stand feeling sad anymore, so I let myself feel angry instead. I'd been blaming Dad moving us here on his waning mental health, but maybe it was just as much about mine.

"I know you don't want to be here, Finn, but this place... it can help, if you let it. It's safe here."

She seemed to genuinely believe that. Perhaps they all did – their chants of safety something they put actual faith into.

"Out there it's all loss and death and danger, but here..." She shook her head, a peaceful smile crossing her lips. "Here we can relax. We won't ever lose anyone again."

Well, that was a delusion if ever I'd heard one. Even if The Retreat kept us safe from electrical fires and beards – whatever bizarre danger Mother believed facial hair held – we were all still going to die sometime. The way Annabelle had said that, though, I could tell she'd lost someone before coming here, just like Dad and I had. So, I kept my mouth shut, having already done enough damage for one day.

Annabelle snapped out of her reverie and unfolded herself from the ground. "I'm going to take you to the health room, so I can bandage your hand and check your nose, then if you would like to join us for dinner, you will be welcome to come to the dining room. You will need to stick to silence though. Mother will remove you again if you don't."

My stomach growled at the mention of the word dinner. "Okay. I mean—" I cut myself off, pressing a finger to my lips.

Annabelle's eyes crinkled. "It will be okay, Finn. You'll see."

She helped me fix my room, then walked me over to the health room. Perhaps I should have felt guilty at accepting her help in tidying a mess I'd made, but I didn't. Her calm presence made it easier – made it feel right. Or not right, exactly, but better than it had been.

She declared my nose unbroken, then bandaged my hand carefully. Her touch was gentle and kind, just like my mum's had been. But I flinched when she brushed my bleeding nails with antiseptic wipes, even as I welcomed the stinging pain. It helped remind me I was real.

I went to leave the room, and she caught my shoulder. "This way, Finn." She turned me around, then glanced back down the corridor in the direction I'd been about to go. I couldn't help but notice the flicker of alarm in her expression. Honestly, I wasn't sure I wanted to know. Whatever secrets or hidden dangers lay that way, The Retreat could keep them.

"Come," she said, a warm smile chasing the anxiety from her face. "I'll walk with you to dinner."

A long, soft flute note rang out, as if in response to her words. Despite myself, I appreciated the melody.

In the dining room, I sat between Mother and Angelina again. There was no sign of Aria, though that wasn't surprising. They had told me I wouldn't be around anyone my own age until I'd acclimated. It would have been helpful if they'd told me the grassy area in the centre of The Retreat was where the kids hung out, though I can't say I would have respected it if they'd said it was off limits.

I wondered about the silence, and the way Mother had clutched at Aria and asked what I'd told her. What did they think I would say to the kids here? What were they so desperate for me to keep quiet about?

Aria, Annabelle, Angelina – odd there were so many A names. Perhaps it was a Retreat thing, and they'd be renaming me Adam or Archibald any moment. The thought made my skin crawl.

Mother smiled at me during the meal; no sign of her earlier anger or fear. Perhaps those emotions weren't good for the soul – perhaps they weren't *safe*. She didn't have to worry about me speaking. I had nothing to say to her.

Annabelle walked me back to my room, and I was glad to have her company over Angelina's. "You did well," she told me.

I opened my mouth to thank her, whether genuinely or sarcastically I wasn't quite sure, but she pressed a finger to her lips. "Silence, remember?"

I frowned, letting out a breath instead of the word.

She patted my arm, sympathetically. "I know it's hard, but it will do you good, I promise. All that grief you're carrying – all that guilt. You can't process it when you block it out with distractions."

Something inside my chest jolted, like her words had physically hit me. Guilt. Did she know, or was she guessing?

"I'd rather have the distractions," I told her.

She grimaced but didn't chide me for speaking. "You think that now, but it will change, Finn. I'll be here when you're ready to set down that burden you're carrying."

I watched her walk away, feeling like an asshole again. I stared out at the compound around me, at the muslin-cloaked figures as they floated around, doing chores. They looked weird, sure, but also... happy? Calm? Peaceful? I didn't know which it was. How could they be happy? How could anyone, cut off from the world like this?

They chatted and laughed as they worked, helping each other. They didn't seem cut off – they seemed connected, touching each other gently in greeting and farewell.

Another lump formed in my throat at that. My mother and Joey had been the only people who ever touched me – Joey in rough and tumble playfights, which Dad yelled at us about, and Mum in affection, hugs and kisses goodnight. After the hugs at the funeral, no one had touched me until Mother clasped my hand between hers.

A cynical puff of air huffed its way through my lips. That much hand holding couldn't be "safe" could it? All that touching would pass on diseases, leaving the whole camp riddled with them. Then again, since they were so isolated from the rest of the world, maybe no one ever got sick.

Here we can relax. We won't ever lose anyone again.

I shook my head. "Bunch of nutters," I said aloud, not caring whether anyone heard.

I slipped inside, and opened the wardrobe door, beginning the ritual of feeding the kittens. Only the dregs of milk and that creamy crust lay in the bottom of the jug, and from the smell of it, it was turning sour. It wasn't surprising, given the cold water could only do so much to keep it fresh.

I would have to find another option – a way to get out of here, or none of us would survive.

Chapter Five

*Y*ou *have to leave... Go get help, Finn. You have to leave...*
I woke in the middle of the night, with my mum's voice floating through my head. My teeth were mashed tight against each other, and my nails dug crescent-shaped wounds into the heels of my palms. I forced my jaw to unclench, and then my hands. Dreaming about the accident always left my body rigid, like some latent version of rigour mortis was taking hold of me, trying to reverse my lucky escape.

Lucky. I hated how people threw that word around. It didn't fit what had happened.

I'd slept only a few fitful hours, and the sky was just beginning to lighten. I lay there for a moment.

Go get help, Finn...

The kittens needed my help. Mum was right, even from beyond the grave.

I hauled myself up and out of the bed, moving quickly. People around here seemed to start the day at sunrise, and I didn't want to give anyone a chance to stop me.

I tossed the latest batch of soiled straw, then headed back to the gate. Annabelle had said the building on the other side of the fence was the kitchen. If there was milk anywhere, it had to be there. Plus, there had to be power. How else would they refrigerate anything? I couldn't imagine Mother was lax about food hygiene, given her obsession with safety.

The padlock held the gate firmly shut this time. I rattled it, but it refused to budge. Beyond the fence, a similar lock barricaded the door of the kitchen building. I groaned and leaned my head against the wire barrier. It pressed into my skin, marking me with the futility of my attempt at caring for another living thing. The kittens were doomed, just like I was. The darkness closed in on me, squeezing the air from my lungs.

"Pull yourself together, Finn," I whispered. I made myself blink, to really look, and make out the shapes of things. "You can still see. It's okay." Faint light trickled from the windows of the building, more evidence of the power inside.

I straightened, brushing myself down. I could do this. Somehow, I could do this. Something caught my eye – a piece of cloth, lit by the hazy illumination from the kitchen windows. Even in that dim glow, I recognised the light blue of denim. I peered at it, willing my pupils to open, to take in as much light as they could, and make the image clear.

It remained dimly murky, but I was sure I recognised the stone-washed fabric – jeans. Mine. My heart hammered at the thought. Mother had to have done something with the clothes she'd confiscated from me. Was this the rubbish? My possessions tossed out beyond the fence to be collected by... god only knew who would trek out here. Perhaps she'd piled everything up ready to burn.

But if my clothes were out there, then maybe my phone was too. I squeezed my fingers tighter around the wire squares of the fence. It was so close – the remnants of my old life, so tantalisingly close, but just beyond my reach.

Come on, Finn. Think.

I let out a breath. If the fence was like the ones at school, then there would be a way out – there had to be. I began a slow walk around the perimeter, forcing myself not to rush, to keep my eyes on the base of the wire. I'd find it – a weak spot in the fence where it hadn't been attached to the ground properly, or the dirt had been kicked away, leaving a gap where the wire could be peeled back like the lid of a sardine can. I'd find it, and I'd slip under.

The sky lightened from charcoal to grey, and I almost turned back. But I couldn't give up, not yet. Then I saw it. The tiniest of gaps at the bottom of the fence. The triangular points of the ends of the wire danced just above the ground as the fence swayed in the breeze.

"You see that, kittens?" I whispered, as if they could hear me from their squalid box in the wardrobe. "I'm going to find you a way out of here." I peeled the fence back as far as it would go – not far – and rolled myself under, taking care not to snag my robes.

I raced back to the rubbish pile, not caring if I made noise, now I was freedom-side. I grabbed the jeans. "Yes!" I whispered. Maybe I cared a little about the noise.

I hugged the jeans to myself, breathing in the familiar scent of washing powder and home. I riffled through the pile of clothes, pulling out one of Dad's shirts and then another of mine.

Laughter escaped my lips, and I hugged the shirts to me too. I'd never thought I was into fashion, nor did I consider myself all that materialistic, but having my own clothes back, having *any* clothes other than these god-awful robes gave me so much hope.

I searched my way through the rest of the pile, pulling out all the familiar items. There was stuff belonging to other people here too – dresses, and a pair of pants I was sure I'd never seen Dad wear. I knew they must be from other recent arrivals – other hapless souls like me and Dad who had been sucked in by the promise of safety. Even so, I couldn't shake the feeling that I was going through the possessions of the deceased. In a way I was. The people who had worn these weren't here anymore. They'd been replaced by marshmallow-wrapped clones, circling these grounds at the behest of Mother. Their old lives were gone, just like mine. Alive and dead, we were all still stuck in the box.

My hand connected with dirt, at the bottom of the pile. No cell phone. Nothing except clothes.

I tried the door of the kitchen building just in case, but the padlock held it firmly closed. *Figures*. It wasn't like there was likely to be anything helpful in there, anyway. The kittens wouldn't be thrilled if I came back with a handful of vegetables for them.

I rubbed my temples, letting out a breath. The clothes were something. They didn't help the kittens, and they certainly didn't get me out of here, but they were still something. I bundled up my favourite items. If I could, I would have taken everything, but I had limited space to hide things, and I couldn't leave the pile looking as if someone had picked through it. I kicked the remaining clothes, heaping them up in an approximation of their original state.

Logically, I knew I should turn back now – take the small victory I'd been given in retrieving something from my old life and get back inside before I was discovered.

I couldn't face it. I wanted just a little longer of freedom, just a little longer to remember who I was.

I walked along beside the river for a while, clutching my pilfered clothing to my chest. It was amazing how much quieter my head was now I was outside the fence. Annabelle was wrong – silence be damned; it was freedom I needed.

The sun would rise in a few hours, and if I wasn't back, no doubt someone would discover I was missing. *Let them*, I thought bitterly. Let them worry I'd been eaten by wild animals. It would shake up their "safe" little world, that was for sure.

I thought about not going back at all – walking or running until I found myself anywhere except on the other side of that fence. But there was Dad, and the stupid box of kittens. Not to mention the fact that I was in the middle of nowhere and would probably starve or die of exposure. I settled for just walking alone beside the river. It wouldn't solve any of my problems, but nor would anything else I had the power to do at the moment.

The river widened out into a deep pool where a tree had grown across its path. That would be blissful later in the day when the sun rose overhead. The leaves would protect me from UV radiation better than any sheet of muslin could – not that I bought into their chant of safety. I stripped off my robes down to my boxers and dove under the water.

Cold, fresh-tasting liquid rushed against my face, and all the tension I'd been holding inside me broke. I laughed. A wired, hysterical sound that was closer to crying came out from deep in my belly. This was all ludicrous, utterly outrageously ludicrous. Surely I would wake up soon, and find this whole bizarre episode – Mother, the marshmallow-coloured clothing, Schrödinger's kittens – had been a dream, as cliché as that sounded.

I laughed until I ran out of breath, then I sank, my mouth filling with water. I let myself drift down into the depths, the weight of the water closing in around me. This was a type of silence I could get behind. I opened my mouth, letting the last gulp of air in my lungs form a bubble which floated up, leaving me behind. Joey's face seemed to dance on its edges, smiling at me. It would be so easy to stay down here. To stop.

I pushed up, and broke the surface, filling my lungs to chase away that thought. I raised my face to the sky, running my hands down it and pretending the liquid I felt around my eyes was just from the river. Of course it wasn't. Of course I was crying again, useless, helpless emotions taking over.

I sank back under, submerging myself.

The whoosh of someone diving in beside me knocked me sideways. I surfaced, sucking in a gasp of air, at the same time taking in a stretch of muslin floating in the water.

"Hello?" I called, forgetting I wasn't allowed to speak.

A face appeared, coughing and spluttering, then arms which flailed and battered at the water. The muslin clung to her, writhing and twisting around her limbs like the hair of some ancient sea hag bent on pulling swimmers to their watery graves.

She went under.

"Hey!" I called, but the girl didn't resurface. I took a deep breath and plunged down after her.

Coils of muslin swarmed in front of me, blocking what little sight I had in the dark water. I reached out, feeling nothing but the seaweed-like swish of the floating fabric. Then, in amongst it, her hand.

I grabbed her, finding her body and slinging my arm around her chest. I kicked upwards, fighting against the clinging muslin, forcing it into a swirling propulsion. We broke the surface, and I floated onto my back, holding her on top of me. She coughed, and flailed against me, panicking still, even though we were on the surface.

"Shh, it's okay. I've got you." I pulled the hair and fabric out of her face so she could breathe, then kicked on my back, dragging her towards the shore.

She didn't open her eyes as I laid her back on the ground, but she moaned slightly, then whispered "thank you." I rolled her onto her side, letting her cough up some of the water she'd swallowed.

"You're all right now."

"You were under the water," she said, her eyes finally opening, dark, just like I knew they would be. "Right under, like the cat. It didn't wake up."

I shivered. I looked out at the water, picturing a drowned cat floating in it. Cats didn't just drown. Someone had done it on purpose.

I guess that was the origin of Schrödinger's kittens.

I looked back at Aria. She stared up at me, still terrified, even though she was back on dry land.

"You're all right now," I said again.

Chapter Six

S he closed her eyes, exhaustion overcoming her. I sat down beside her, looking at the water. It didn't seem so peaceful now I knew a cat had drowned here – had *been* drowned here.

"What were you doing in the water?" she asked me, her voice breathy as her chest figured out it was safely back on dry land. "Did you fall in?"

"No, I jumped in. Why did you follow me if you can't swim?"

She opened her eyes, frowning at me. "Swim?" She pronounced the word uncertainly, as if she'd never heard it before.

"You know... swimming." I curved my arms over my head, one after the other, mimicking freestyle strokes.

Her frown deepened, a wariness growing in her eyes. I stopped flailing, the movement clearly meaning nothing to her. "It doesn't matter," I said weakly, embarrassment taking over.

She shivered, her gaze sliding back to the water. "I thought you were going to go to sleep – the bad sleep, I mean. Like the cat."

It was my turn to frown. There was something odd about the way she was speaking. Did she not know the word "drown"? I guess that made sense if she didn't know swimming, but did she maybe not even know the word "death" either? Or was she just afraid to say it?

"I wanted to make you safe," she said quietly, perhaps unnerved by my silence.

I cleared my throat. There it was again – safe. They all seemed to know that word. "Thank you," I said. "I'm okay. I'm safe in the water. You're not, though. You should stay out of it."

I stuck to simple sentences, hoping she would understand, but a part of me felt bad. I didn't want to treat her like she was stupid. She just nodded, her expression solemn. I got the feeling she heard speeches about safety a lot.

"How did you get out here?" I asked.

Her lips twitched. "There's a gap under the fence. I come out at night sometimes. No one knows."

I smiled. I was right, she wasn't stupid. She was clever – sneaky – even if she was stuck in this creepy place.

She sat up suddenly, staring at me accusingly. "I'm not supposed to talk to you."

I raised my eyebrows. "You're also not supposed to sneak out or hide boxes of cats either."

She frowned. "True." She worried at her lip with her teeth. "You're not going to tell anyone, are you?"

I stared at her, shocked by the question. She stared back, genuine concern pinching her gaze.

"Of course not," I told her. "I'm out here too, remember?"

She let out a breath, and the corners of her lips twitched again, almost but not quite turning into a smile. That was interesting. Everyone here seemed to have smiles sewn into their faces – the peaceful vagueness like a uniform they all wore from the moment they woke. Aria's face was more expressive – more serious. I had a feeling when she did smile, it was always genuine.

"We just need to get back before sunup, except..." She looked down at her robes, hanging off her in sodden trails, and her face fell. She pulled them from herself, exposing flashes of bare skin underneath.

"Um... what are you doing?" I asked.

"I need to get this off. It has to dry before I go back."

"Okay, but don't..."

She pulled the whole thing over her head, and to my horror – and not horror, if you get what I mean – she was naked underneath, bar a pair of pale undies. I stared, my eyes going wide, taking in her body. Then I swear I heard my mother's voice scream at me from beyond the grave.

I closed my eyes, turning away, though everything in me wanted to keep staring. Well, maybe not everything, but one particular part of me, not very well protected by my still wet boxers.

"What's wrong?" she asked, absolute innocence in her voice.

What the actual fuck was going on here? How sheltered was this girl's life that she didn't know how to swim, let alone that she shouldn't strip in front of a guy she didn't know?

"Nothing," I choked out. "Nothing's wrong. You shouldn't get cold, though. There're some things you can wear over there." I gestured at the pile of clothes I'd rescued.

She was like a child – a little innocent kid. That thought put a welcome damper on things. I risked a glance down at myself. My boxers still clung to my skin, offering me no protection. "And can you hand me my jeans? Uh... the blue pants," I added, hazarding a guess that she might not know the name for those either.

"Okay. You're being weird, though," she said, a laugh in her voice. I joined her, laughing a little too loudly. She tapped my arm with the jeans, and I took them from her without turning around, pulling them on quickly.

"Are you dressed yet?" I asked her.

"Yes. These clothes are strange though."

I let out another too-loud laugh at that and turned back to her. Jesus, the girl still wasn't dressed properly. She'd pulled on a pair of my shorts, and one of Dad's shirts. She hadn't done up the buttons though, letting it hang open down the front, barely covering her.

"You need to do up the buttons," I said, gesturing to them.

She glanced down, patting the shirt. Seriously? She didn't know the word buttons either? She found the plastic circles but fumbled with them, clearly unfamiliar with the concept after however many years of shapeless robes.

"How?" She looked up at me.

I almost told her to leave it – figured I'd just do my best not to look at her chest lest my dead mother start yelling at me again. Then, I saw something in her face. She wanted to know, not just because I was telling her she had to get dressed, but because an excitement was lighting inside of her at the idea of something new. No wonder, if her life had been this controlled.

I stepped forward, taking one of the buttons in my hand. "It goes through this little hole, see?" I did up the button for her. My cheeks reddened as the back of my hand brushed against her breast. I stepped backwards, folding my hands into my armpits. "You can do the rest."

She moved the button across slowly, concentrating hard as she pushed it through the buttonhole. Her face lit up at her success, an actual full smile appearing. "I think I remember this…" She frowned, the memory seeming to slip away from her. "From a long time ago."

I nodded. "Cool. Do the rest of them."

My mother's voice started yelling again at that. Aria shouldn't have to be covered up for me not to perve at her. Mum had taught me better than that. But seriously? Mum hadn't expected a strange girl to get naked in front of me with no understanding of what it meant.

Aria didn't protest, clearly enjoying practising her new-found skill.

I focused on her face. Her hair was long, and curly like mine, though the water stretched it out into long ropes. I wondered how I hadn't noticed the curls before, but of course the hood had kept it covered. With our similar eyes and skin tone, we could practically be brother and sister. That thought made me uncomfortable enough to make the whole open shirt thing way easier.

She did the buttons up wonky, matching them sideways into the wrong holes, but it didn't matter. She looked up at me when she finished, her expression bright.

"Good job," I said, as if I were talking to Joey.

"Can you help me hang this up?" she asked, gesturing to her robe.

"Yeah, sure."

We slung it between two trees, but the early morning air was more or less still, and the sun not up yet. "I don't think it will dry before sunrise though."

"It has to." Aria's voice rose, a crack of desperation running through it. "I've never been caught before. I can't explain wet robes."

Again, I wondered at the fact that she had crept out. So innocent – naïve – yet she still felt the urge to crawl under that fence. The urge to break free.

She looked as if she might cry, her eyes wide and shadowed. She still shivered from her brush with drowning, or as she would have put it, her brush with the bad sleep. I cast my gaze around, looking for anything that would help us dry off faster. Instead, my eye landed on my own robe, folded up neatly on the bank where I'd left it.

"Are there any differences between the men's and women's robes?" I asked her.

She shook her head. "I don't think so."

"Then you can wear mine." I picked it up and handed it to her. Thankfully, she didn't immediately strip again to put it on.

She hesitated. "Then what will you wear?"

I shrugged. "My boxers. Or I can wear the wet one."

"But then they'll know you snuck out."

I shrugged again, honestly not caring. "So?" Then again, if they caught me, they would find the hole in the fence, and that would put an end to either of us sneaking out. And it would mean losing my chance to help the kittens. "I'll toss it in the shower when I get back. They'll think I was just having a tantrum and lock me in my room, or something. They won't know we were outside."

Her shoulders dropped an inch, relaxing a little at the idea. She nodded. "That could work." She unravelled my robe, examining it. "It's the wrong colour, but if I avoid Mother until I can change it, I don't think anyone else will remember which one I wore yesterday."

The implication being that Mother would remember what colour anyone wore on any given day. I didn't think that woman could get any creepier.

I glanced around at the river, and the swimming hole created by the fallen branch. Under different circumstances, I could imagine coming back here in the daytime, maybe even teaching Aria to swim, both of us splashing and laughing in the water, just like Joey and I had always done. I shook my head, brushing my little sister's image away.

"There's still the problem of the kittens," I said.

"Kittens..." She hesitated over the word.

"Baby cats?" I tried. God, this was weird. Maybe English wasn't her first language. She didn't have an accent exactly, or at least not one I recognised, though she spoke slowly, drawing out the vowels sometimes as she thought words over.

"Oh..." Her face brightened in recognition but then clouded again. "You didn't take care of them?"

"Yeah, I have been, but I can't keep them in a box forever. The whole wardrobe is starting to stink, and I'm nearly out of milk." Not to mention how the milk was starting to stink too. It was surprising I hadn't been caught just from that, but perhaps Mother was one of those people who thought teenage boys always smelled bad, even when she was making me shower and shave every morning.

"I can get more milk," Aria said, ignoring my other complaints.

"Where did they come from?"

Aria frowned and her shoulders hunched up. "I found the cat out here and brought it inside. I don't know where the little ones came from. They just appeared."

I nodded, not filling in the blank for her. It didn't surprise me no one had taught her where babies came from. In fact, it explained quite a bit. "And then the cat di—" I cut myself off. "And then the cat... went to sleep?"

Aria shrunk before my eyes, her whole body closing in on itself. "Mother found them. She made Angelina take them away." She looked out at the water, her face haunted. "That's how I found out what they're called. She yelled, 'Don't you know how dangerous it is bringing a cat in here, Aria! Cats aren't safe!' Then Angelina took them out through the gate. I found the cat in the water that night."

I stepped towards her, touching her arm gently. "It's okay, you don't have to talk about it."

Aria didn't seem to hear me. She shivered, still staring out over the water. Even without having seen it, the image of the cat's floating body drew a swirling nausea into my stomach. If she had no understanding of life and death, it must have been terrifying for her.

"Then you found the kittens, though, right?" However it happened, that had to have been a better mental picture. "You did good saving them."

She nodded, the horror not leaving her face. "I heard them crying; she'd left them in a hole."

Without really meaning to, I was stroking her arm, soothing her in the way my mother would have done for me when something awful happened. Aria relaxed under my touch, her hunched shoulders slowly softening. Perhaps there was something to all this physical contact The Retreat insisted upon.

"I hid them in the empty room. But then Mother said you were coming, and—"

"And you slipped me the note. That was clever."

Slipping me the note *was* clever, but I hoped I would have taken care of the kittens regardless – that I wasn't the sort of asshole who'd have abandoned them if I hadn't specifically been asked to give a shit.

Aria looked up at the sky, and I followed her gaze. The grey of the night was shifting, patches of an anaemic yellow creeping in. "We should get back," she said. "We don't have long."

"Yeah."

She started to unbutton the shirt, and I turned away, gathering up the clothing I'd reclaimed. I grabbed her sodden robe too, ready to enact our plan of feigning a minor act of destructive disobedience. Honestly, the idea of leaving a soaking robe in the shower gave me some pleasure. I just wished I'd thought of dumping one in there earlier.

I turned around, and fortunately Aria was fully clothed now, back in the ridiculous folds of muslin fabric. She took my hand, squeezing it. "Thank you, Finn. For pulling me out." She glanced back at the water, troubled tension crossing her face. She looked back at me. "It you hadn't... would I...?" She didn't finish the thought, and I shook my head, not wanting to be the one to tell her she and everyone around her was going to die someday.

"Don't worry about that. We have to get back."

She nodded, dragging her eyes away from the water.

Chapter Seven

We slipped under the fence, just as the sun began to creep over the hills. I heard a clunk, then a whoosh as the power turned back on.

"We're too late." Aria's voice was barely above a whisper. "We'll be caught. I can't do another night in the repercussion rooms, I just can't!"

Repercussion rooms... That's where Mother had sent the man who punched me.

I shook my head. "*You* won't be caught. Just me." I don't know what it was that made me feel responsible for her. Perhaps the fact that she'd jumped into the water to save me, even when she couldn't swim herself, or perhaps that her helpless innocence reminded me so much of my little sister. I swallowed a lump in my throat.

"Here." I bundled my pile of reclaimed clothes into her arms. "Can you hide these somewhere? And don't forget the milk for the kittens." I slipped off my jeans, returning to just my boxers, and added the jeans to the pile.

She nodded, pulling me into a hug. "Thank you."

The bare skin on my chest turned to gooseflesh under her touch, and I inhaled, breathing in the scent of her wet hair. It took everything in me not to pull her closer. Instead, I stepped back and pushed her towards the dining room just as the doors to the dormitories began to open.

"Go. Say you woke up early and went for a walk around the grounds." I wasn't sure whether that was allowed, but it would sure be better than them knowing she'd been outside the fence.

I turned away, not waiting for an answer. I ran to the middle of the compound, yell-singing as loud as I could. "I'm doing something naughty. I'm doing something naugh-ty." It was what Joey and I used to do when we knew we were already in trouble. Nine times out of ten, it would make Mum laugh enough to let us off without punishment.

"I'm doing something naughty!"

It was working. The people exiting the dormitories watched me instead of Aria. She disappeared around the side of the dining hall, and I dashed towards the bathrooms. I could already sense people starting to follow me, and I had to be quick to make this convincing. I dumped Aria's sodden robes in the bottom of the shower, turning it on full blast.

The murky river water rose up, obviously not from the taps, and folds of fabric blocked the drain. "Shit." I kicked it sideways, letting the water swirl away. A few seconds more and the dirty water began to clear until it could pass as having come from my small act of destruction.

The door flew open. Angelina stared at me, her hair and movements wild, no sign of the floaty, peaceful swish-glide now. "Finn," she breathed, voice still soft. "What on earth are you doing?"

I shrugged, a little smirk crawling across my face.

"I..." Angelina shook her head, her mouth gaping as she tried to find words. "You'll have to speak to Mother," she said finally.

I nodded. "Yeah, that seems about right."

She shook her head once more, then finally had the sense to shut off the water. I surveyed the results. As minor destruction went, it had been pretty effective. The robe had slithered its way back to the plug hole and blocked it up again. Just a few more minutes with the showerhead running full blast and the whole bathroom would have been flooded.

"Come." Angelina grabbed my arm, pulling me from the bathroom, no gentleness in her tone or her touch this time. Members of The Retreat had gathered outside, drawn by the sudden noise. They gawked at me, at my bare chest and spindly legs in my boxer shorts. I waved, grinning at them. Given they were forced into those robes day in day out, this was probably the most skin any of them had seen in years.

I caught sight of Annabelle, her hand pressed to her mouth. Around it, her eyes crinkled, and her shoulders shook with laughter just like Mum's would have.

Behind her – behind the crowd – a figure crept, making her way from the dining room to my bedroom, hopefully with a big jug of stolen milk.

"I did something naugh-ty," I sang out, keeping everyone's focus on me. "I did something naughty."

"Hush... why can't you just be safe?" Angelina whispered to me.

I shook my head. It wasn't *my* safety I was worried about.

I SAT CROSS LEGGED on the hessian floor mat of Mother's office, yes, still in my damp boxers. I was starting to regret that part.

I hadn't really looked around properly the last time I'd been in here, too focused on my dad and the breakdown he must be having to have brought us to this god-awful place. If I was honest, the room was actually pleasant – calming. A light breeze blew in from the cracked window, bringing with it a soft scent of... something. Honeysuckle, maybe. Mum would have known.

The creamy coloured walls and gentle warmth made me feel sleepy; that soft, safe feeling like being little and curled up in a blanket on my mother's lap.

I shivered, pushing the thought away. I couldn't get comfortable here.

Finally, the door opened, and Mother and Angelina wafted in. Angelina's gait had returned to her drugged-like drift, and her face to a vague blissed-out expression. She handed me a new robe. "Don't get cold, Finn," she said, her voice – you guessed it – back to the calm, musical lilt.

She touched Mother's arm. Mother returned the gesture, so they were crossed at the elbows, and then Angelina left the room, closing the door softly behind her.

Mother stood for a moment. She leaned back ever so slightly, her eyes closed as if enjoying the lumbar stretch. Then she straightened, her gaze landing on me. The last shreds of excitement I'd felt this morning fled, and a chilly fear crept into its place. It wasn't that her gaze was angry, if anything it was bland, expressionless, almost. The creepy part was that she didn't blink. Didn't smile. She did nothing but stare at me.

"I'm sorry," I said.

"No, you're not."

She was right; I wasn't, but it's what you say, isn't it? And then adults forgive you, because you're just a teenager, and teenagers make stupid mistakes.

The mental image of the drowned cat floated into my mind, and I shivered. I'd seen Mother as harmless, an adversary to be toyed with but not feared. Yet, she had taken a living thing and ordered one of her staff to do that to it. What kind of person could be that cruel?

"Put your robe on. You're cold."

It wasn't the chill making me shiver, but I put the robe on anyway, for once glad of the soft folds of fabric brushing against my skin.

"I've been very patient with you, Finn," she said, her voice even.

I nodded. She had, or she hadn't drowned me at least. I'd been right to protect Aria this morning. The girl didn't understand the danger she was in – that we were all in.

Mother sighed, then folded herself up, sitting down in front of me. "You are an unusual case. I let you and your father come here because your story touched me."

I frowned, watching her face for any hints of deception. She'd said that before, touching her chest in a fake gesture of emotion that didn't reach her eyes. This time, her voice sounded more genuine, but I didn't know whether to trust her. She had to have a reason for bringing us here; I just wasn't sure that was it.

"People normally come here by choice. They understand we can help them. Like your father – he wants to be here."

"Dad doesn't know what he wants," I said.

Surprisingly, Mother nodded. "Most people don't."

I guess that was true. Until recently, I'd thought adults had it all figured out. As soon as Mum and Joey died, it was like a light switch turned on, and I'd been desperately trying to get back to the dark ever since. When I could see them clearly, when their faces were fully illuminated, it was obvious that most adults were terrified, and I would give anything to go back to not knowing that.

"Normally, if someone was this unhappy, they would be withdrawn from The Retreat."

A surge of hope rose in my chest. She would send me and Dad home? I studied her face, waiting for her to say the words. She studied me right back, a tiny line appearing between her eyebrows.

If someone was this unhappy. Some*one*, singular. Dad *was* happy here; she meant just me.

"I'm not going to do that, today. I still believe we can help you, Finn, that *I* can help you. I think, if you are honest with yourself, you want that too. So, I'm going to keep you here. I'm going to keep you safe."

The bubble of hope in my chest burst with a painful pop. No escape for me or Dad. But would I have wanted to leave on my own? I thought about the question, and truthfully, the answer was yes. If I could get back to civilisation, to Carly and my other friends, to normal clothes and freedom, I would be racing towards it, even if Dad didn't follow me.

I didn't want to abandon him. He might think he was happy, but how could he be, really, living under the rule of a cat-killer. Hell, I didn't even want to leave Aria here, and I'd only properly met her half a day ago. But I had to get out.

The way Aria talked scared me. Her confusion, and lack of education on the most basic of subjects – that had to be some type of child abuse, right?

"Why don't you want me to talk to anyone?" The question spilled through my lips, before I'd really even heard it form in my mind. I already thought I had an answer, but I wanted to see what Mother would say.

Mother sighed. Her eyes drifted away from mine, looking out the window at the people outside. "I built this place after my son died," she said softly.

Her face drew in, pinching at the memory, and she stared into space as if staring through time. I swear, if I'd followed her gaze right in that moment, I would have seen through time too, but not to her car accident – to mine.

Mother took a breath, dragging herself back to the present. "There are many who have been with me since the beginning. Many whose children were born here or came when they were very young."

I nodded. Like Aria, I guessed.

"They don't know of the world – of its ugliness and danger."

I nodded again, though it wasn't true. Aria had seen ugliness right here.

"I... I want to keep it that way. You understand?"

I did. Even if the execution had been horrible, I could see she had a noble goal at heart.

"If you promise not to tell them..." Mother's words were almost whispers. "Promise to protect them from the world... then you may speak."

I blinked at her. I hadn't expected this. I thought I'd come out of this meeting and be sent straight to my room, locked in there for the rest of my so-called acclimation period. Perhaps Mother understood more than I'd given her credit for. Perhaps she knew my small act of vandalism was just the beginning, and she needed to work with me, not against me, or she would lose.

"Okay," I said. It didn't feel like a lie. I would tell Aria about the world, but I planned to leave out the ugly parts. She needed an education, but no one needed that.

Chapter Eight

Angelina escorted me back to my room. A little kick had added itself to the end of each of her swish-glide steps, and I could tell she would rather Mother had withdrawn me from The Retreat. *Joke's on you, Angelina.* That's what I'd wanted too.

True to her word, Mother had given me back some level of freedom in exchange for my promise to keep the world from the children here. Angelina didn't turn away when I thanked her for walking me back, and she didn't lock the door behind her when she left. Still, I let out a long breath once she'd gone, only able to fully relax now I was alone.

I closed my eyes, tempted to curl up on the bed and sleep, making up for the wandering hours of the night. Something I couldn't quite put my finger on niggled at the back of my mind, something that wasn't right...

I opened my eyes with a lurch. The kittens. No plaintive mewing had greeted me when I walked in the door, and only silence filled the air around me now. I'd left them too long – taken too long to find Aria and failed in finding them more milk. I moved towards the wardrobe. The floorboards creaked underfoot in a painful parody of the kittens' cries. Seconds passed, but I couldn't do it. I couldn't open the door and see their bodies still and lifeless. God, I was ready to cry now, even without seeing that.

Come on, Finn, I told myself. *They're okay. They'll be okay.*

I opened the door, careful not to shake the wardrobe. I peeked into the box. Eight sleeping furballs piled on top of each other, their little chests rising and falling almost in sync. "Hey little dudes," I whispered.

A new, full jug of milk sat on the shelf, a bowl of ice surrounding it. As for the kittens, they smelled fresher. Their bedding was clean, and even the box had been replaced – I didn't recognise the writing on the side, though I couldn't say I'd looked that closely earlier. Aria must have fed them too, as they were sleeping soundly, their bellies round and full.

"She really cares about you, little fluffballs, doesn't she?" How had she managed this? Sneaking back into the building was one thing, but somehow, she'd managed to organise all this too. My stunt with the robes in the bathrooms must have really held everyone's attention. I supposed it wasn't something they saw often, if Mother was right and everyone else was here by choice.

"I'm going to find a way to get you out of here, fluffballs," I told the kittens. I didn't know how yet, but having Aria on my side gave me just that little bit more confidence I could do it.

ANNABELLE FETCHED ME for lunch. I knew the way to the dining hall by now, but I was happy to see her regardless.

"Are you well, Finn?" she asked as we walked.

I nodded. The familiar lines creased around her eyes at my wordless answer, and I found myself smiling too. "I'm well," I said.

"Good," she said. "I'm glad to see you safe."

My smile fell at that. Always this obsession with safety, even if it came at the cost of something else. The poor cat. Somehow, Mother and Angelina would pay for that.

"Are you hungry?" Annabelle asked.

My stomach growled in response. "Starving." I'd missed breakfast and my guts weren't happy about it. I didn't mind eating vegetarian meals – preferred them, even – but I still wasn't used to having someone else dictate my mealtimes. I missed having a kitchen, a supply of food I could dive into whenever I felt the need.

"Good," Annabelle said as we reached the dining hall door. "Go eat and talk. Food and conversation are both good for the soul."

I nodded, though I wasn't sure I agreed. The food might help my soul, or at the very least my belly, but conversation with Mother would only serve to build the rough edges of the anger grating underneath my skin.

I made my way across the dining hall. I cast my eye over each of the people I passed. Aria wasn't there, of course, or at least I couldn't spot her in the crowd of muslin-covered figures.

"Finn, over here." Mother beckoned me to her table.

I hesitated, then continued on towards her, barely breaking my stride. So I was still expected to sit between Mother and Angelina, my hippie body guards. Or perhaps prison guards would be more accurate. To them, I was the danger, not the one to be protected. While Mother was giving me more freedom, she'd still be keeping me apart from her precious born-here children for as long as she could. At least until I acclimated, whatever that meant. It sounded suspiciously like brain-washing.

Mother smiled as I sat down beside her, and I forced my lips to curve into something that could pass as a smile in response. The food had already been served, but I knew to wait for Mother's prayer.

She and Angelina took my hands. "Together we breathe; together we are safe."

"Together we breathe; together we are safe," the congregation echoed back.

I inhaled with them, without meaning to. Mother smiled as I did, and finally, we could eat.

"Did you have a safe morning?" Mother asked me.

I nodded. "Yeah... I had a good morning." I actually had. Successfully getting Aria back inside had lifted my spirits, and seeing the kittens happy and fed made me feel better too. Of course, I couldn't tell Mother about any of that.

"I'm glad. It's nice to see you starting to acclimate at last."

I took another mouthful of food so I didn't have to answer that ridiculous statement. Beside me, Angelina sniffed, then let out a little cough. Neither action did anything to hide her displeasure. She smiled at me blandly, pretending to agree.

It's okay, chick, I wanted to say. *I know as well as you do that I ain't acclimating at all.*

I chewed my way through another mouthful of... something. Don't get me wrong, it didn't taste bad, but all the food here had the same vegetable mash texture. It reminded me of baby food.

"What is this?" I asked Angelina.

"Vegetable stew."

Well, that I should have been able to guess. I wasn't used to it being so... pureed though. Angelina seemed to sense I needed more explanation. "All our meals are prepared to give the best nutritional content. And the texture is carefully managed to reduce choking hazard. Mother thinks of everything to keep us safe."

I stared at her, and she stared back, her face returning to the blissed-out peaceful expression. There was no hint of sarcasm in the way she'd said that, completely earnest in her belief that feeding us all baby food was a completely normal and rational thing for Mother to be doing. I didn't think choking hazards were something able-bodied people had to think about after the age of five.

"Well, okay then," I said.

I wondered what Dad thought of this. He'd been a meat and three veg kind of guy my whole life, and he loved a good lasagne. I couldn't see him lapping up this mush, no matter how indoctrinated he was into Mother's world of safety.

The widespread baby proofing certainly hadn't worked when it came to Aria. She'd have drowned if I hadn't been there this morning. Or would she? She hadn't known the word "swimming". Maybe the plan was that if she didn't know about it, she'd never try to enter the water, never even go near it if she stayed on this side of the fence. That didn't seem a terribly reliable plan. My parents had taken me to swimming lessons as a kid, not because they wanted me in the water, but because they knew that one way or another, I'd find my way into it, and they may not have been there to fish me out.

I cast my eye around the room once more, searching for Aria. She still didn't materialise. I wish I'd made some plan to meet up with her, or at least got her to give me some clue as to where she'd hidden my clothes. I did know one thing, though. She'd got out of the compound through the same hole in the fence that I had, and it wasn't the first time she'd gone wandering at night. I brightened at that, the thought setting a warm glow flickering inside me. We didn't have a plan, but I still had a way to find her.

AS SOON AS I HEARD the clunk of the power turning off, and the room around me fell into darkness, I itched to be outside, to race to the fence and peel it back, disappearing out into the night. I forced myself to wait, wait, wait for the others to settle, to fall asleep as the night pressed upon them.

I'd already fed the kittens. They'd lapped up the new milk greedily, far more eager than they'd been for the souring dregs I'd been giving them. I wondered again where it came from. The camp wasn't vegan. I'd seen fresh eggs in our meals – mashed, of course, to meet the texture requirements – and occasionally tasted cheese in amongst the pureed food. Vegetables were grown on the land, everyone chipping in to tend to them, but there were no farm animals in sight.

That was another thing I'd need to ask Aria about, though I suspected she wouldn't know the answer.

Judging time was difficult without a watch or phone. I waited for what I estimated was about an hour, then creaked my bedroom door open. Crickets and other night-time sounds swirled around me, a sure sign that the bigger, human life had stilled. I closed the door behind me, and crept across the compound, keeping to the shadows.

I retraced my steps from the gate, noting the hum of electricity coming from the kitchen building. I almost missed the gap under the fence. The points of the wire were so close to the ground, it would be easy to assume they were attached. Perfect. That was the way I liked it: an escape route that didn't leave an obvious trail.

I slipped underneath, taking care with my robes. A repeat of this morning's performance wouldn't go down well, and I didn't want to have to get inventive, finding another way to explain wet or damaged clothes. I scrambled up and looked around, as if Aria would be right in front of me, somehow invisible from the other side of the fence despite the hole-pocked mesh of its wire.

She wouldn't stop here. She was smarter than that, even if I didn't appear to be. I slid between the trees, following the river back to the pool.

"Aria?" I whispered, once I was far enough away from the fence to risk it.

At first, only crickets answered me, then a rustle silenced them. "Finn?" she called back, softly. "I'm over here."

I moved towards her voice, conscious of the darkness hiding all manner of things. I imagined spindly fingers stretching out to wrap around my ankles... or just staying stationary and letting my clumsy feet trip over them. I'd been right to wait for the early hours of the morning last time. My city eyes hadn't evolved to trek easily through the dark of real wilderness.

I heard a breath, and the outline of Aria's body became clear in front of me, the light of the moon catching on her hair.

She found my hand, pulling me close to her. "You came. I was scared you wouldn't."

We sat, carefully, on a fallen log. She didn't let go of my hand. Her fingers were icy against mine, and I felt her shiver. How long had she been out here? Had she left the compound as soon as the power had gone out?

"I wanted to make sure everyone was asleep," I told her.

She shifted – a nod perhaps, or maybe moving closer – then another breath. I felt the heat of her exhale against my neck, and I shivered a different type of shiver.

"Everyone falls asleep pretty much straight away. It's boring once the lights go out, and Mother doesn't allow talking."

Unsurprising. I bet she liked to monitor conversations between her sheep, and that was easier in the light.

"Did you bring those clothes?" she asked. "They're warmer than the robes."

"I thought you had them."

"I hid them under your bed. I thought you'd look."

I let out a little laugh. I should have, but I'd been busy with the kittens. "I got the milk," I told her. "How did you manage all that without being seen?"

She shifted again, away this time. "I had help," she said, hesitancy lining her voice. "There's one other person who knows about the kittens. Don't ask me who."

Her tone was final, a hard protectiveness coming down in a barrier around her co-conspirator. I squeezed her hand, pouring reassurance into the touch. "It's okay. I won't ask. I don't know anyone else here anyway."

That wasn't entirely true. I knew Mother and Angelina, but I couldn't see either of them helping. Annabelle... maybe. She was hard to figure out.

"We can get more when the kittens need it," Aria said. "You just need to tell me when."

"Thanks, but they won't be able to live on milk forever. We need a plan for them." After finding out what had happened to their mother, I wasn't sure about the idea of releasing them into the wild. I had visions of Mother rounding them up and... I never let the vision get past that point.

"What do they need to eat?" Aria asked.

"Cat biscuits... meat." I'd never actually owned a cat, but I was pretty sure I'd read they couldn't survive on a vegetarian diet. Something about them needing amino acids only found in the violence of carnivore life.

"Meat..." Aria pronounced the word slowly, another unfamiliar one,

"Um... like steak, chicken, pork... fish, maybe."

Her silence told me she wasn't getting it. I sighed. "Animals. Uh... dead ones." I didn't censor the word this time, but I think the meaning was pretty damn clear.

"To eat?!" Her voice shot up, and I shushed her, glancing nervously back towards the compound. "Do all cats do that?" she asked, disgust curling the edges of her words.

"Cats... most humans. It's not as bad as it sounds." Or it was, but we tried not to think too hard about it.

I could practically see Aria's stomach curdling at the thought, and I didn't dare tell her she had most likely eaten meat too before her parents brought her to The Retreat. Unless she was one of the ones born here. I rushed on, before she could ask the next obvious question – had *I* ever eaten dead animals.

"I think I have an idea," I told her. A plan had seeded itself in my mind this afternoon, but there were a few key components missing before it would grow. "I need your help."

Aria took a breath. "Of course."

She was so trusting, but of course she was. She probably didn't know untrustworthy people existed. If her world hadn't been blown up by Mother and that cat, she could have gone on thinking all humans were good. For a moment, I saw the appeal – a quiet life, sheltered from harm.

Then again, she wasn't sheltered. She was controlled, and she would always be in danger with Mother in charge.

"I have a friend back home. I think she would come get the kittens if I asked her to." That wasn't the only reason I wanted to contact Carly, of course, and a small twinge of guilt tweaked at the back of my skull. Was I manipulating Aria, by asking for her help in this?

Yes, I concluded. I was. But was it for good reasons? Well, that remained to be seen.

"Someone from outside?" Aria's voice went small, child-like. What had Mother told her about us – about outsiders? She had to have seen people coming into the camp, but if Mother kept them away until they'd acclimated, maybe she never saw anything that gave her clues that we were still people, just like her.

"A friend," I said again. "She's a good person. I think you would like her." I honestly did. Aria reminded me a lot of Carly – she was just as smart and brave, just as strong. She didn't have

Carly's sarcastic tongue, though, but that wasn't surprising, given where she'd grown up.

Aria shifted uneasily, unconvinced. She was still here, still listening. That was something.

"How would you tell her, though?" she asked. "We never see anyone from outside."

That couldn't be true. There had to be deliveries sometimes, otherwise, where did the eggs come from? Or the thousands of metres of muslin it must take to make these robes.

"I had a phone when I arrived. It wasn't with my clothes. I think Mother might still have it."

Aria shook her head, the ends of her hair brushing my arm. "A phone...?"

I sighed. Of course, she wouldn't know what that was. "It's a thin, black plastic and metal box," I said. My English teacher back home would be shaking her head at my lack of descriptive skills. "About this big." I gestured with my hands, uselessly, given the dark. "It lights up sometimes – makes noises."

"Oh..." Aria made a humming sound, thinking. "I have seen something like that, maybe. There's a cupboard in Mother's office, where she keeps stuff like that. Stuff from outside."

Take that, English teachers! Aria had recognised my rubbish description. "Could you get me in there?"

Aria tilted her head back and forth in something somewhere between a nod and a shake. Her whole body swayed with the movement, brushing against me. "Maybe... it would be difficult though."

"For the kittens, could you?" That was definitely manipulative of me, unkind even, but I had to get out of here. I had to get *us* out of here. Aria might not realise it yet, but she was going to have to leave. Maybe not with me, but eventually. A girl like her – adventurous, curious – wouldn't last long without getting into trouble in a place like this. The cat was just a taste of what trouble could look like.

"Yes," Aria said. "For the kittens, I could do it."

A tight little knot formed in my stomach, joining all of the other firmly bound knots of guilt I had stored in there. It didn't matter. If we got out, it would be worth it.

"But not tonight," Aria said, and I nodded.

"No, not tonight."

She stood, brushing off her robe as if she had done this many times before. "I'll need time to plan. I'll contact you when I'm ready, or my friend will."

I stood too, our bodies close in the dark. I didn't step away. "Will I see you again, though? Tomorrow night?"

She started to shake her head, but then nodded, the ends of her hair dancing over my skin again. "Tomorrow. Straight after lights out." She leaned forward, and for a moment I thought she might be about to kiss me. Instead, she placed her hands on my shoulders in the same way they all seemed to do here. From her, it felt different.

And then she was gone, stepping back into the night and disappearing into the darkness. "Wait a little before you follow." Her voice came floating back to me. "And go slowly. Don't make too much noise."

Like I said, she was smart. I waited, but there were no more instructions, the sounds of night creeping back in to fill the absence our finished conversation had left.

Chapter Nine

The day felt interminably long. I fed the kittens, I helped harvest vegetables, I pretended to get a drink so I could steal more ice. Twice, I reached for my phone to check the time. Twice, my hand smacked against my thigh without encountering a pocket let alone a device. Was this why girls always excitedly announced when their dresses had pockets? I vowed to never take them for granted again. If I ever got out of here that was.

After dinner, I could barely wait for lights out to go meet Aria. I couldn't believe I'd wasted so much time the night before.

When the power clunked out, I pulled two sweaters on over my robe, then counted my breaths. I'd read twelve per minute was about average. I quickly did the maths, reckoning ninety-six breaths or eight minutes was a good compromise between giving people time to fall asleep and me not tearing my own hair out with the wait.

I lost count somewhere in the sixties.

Screw it. That was long enough.

I crept out, following the lines of the buildings then dodging over to the fence. Aria materialised out of the darkness as I reached The Retreat's perimeter.

"Hey," I whispered.

She pressed a finger to my lips, then made a series of random gestures I could only just see in the dim light. It didn't matter. They were bound to mean the equivalent of *shut up before we get caught and follow me under the fence.*

I held the ends of the wire up while she rolled under, then she did the same for me. She crouched down once I was safely on the other side, and bent the loose wires back into place, then scuffed up the dirt, getting rid of the smooth patch where we'd rolled through. Smart. The girl knew how to cover her tracks.

She took my hand, pulling me towards the river.

We made our way out to where we'd sat before. I took the top sweater off, handing it to her. "This will keep you warm," I said.

"Thank you." She pulled it on over her head.

I frowned. It suddenly occurred to me that I could see a lot better than the night before, despite the darkness. I looked up at the full moon above our heads.

"Where I come from, there are all sorts of superstitions about the full moon," I said.

She frowned. "Super...?"

"Like things people believe? Scary stuff usually." That wasn't a good explanation, given most of her daily life could fit into that category. Was that how Mother had started out? Her belief system seemed to be a strange mix of half-understood science and outright nonsense.

"What do people believe?" Aria asked. "About the moon."

I leaned back on my elbows so I could look at it. After a moment, Aria did the same, stretching out her legs to lie beside me.

"They say it makes people crazy... that strange things happen. That it's a time when witches are most powerful. Then of course there are werewolves..." I glanced at her. "People who turn into wolves on the full moon."

I realised too late that if she hadn't known what cats were, there was no way she was going to have heard of wolves.

She didn't ask, shaking her head instead. "There's so much I don't know about the outside world."

I gave a half laugh. "This isn't the important stuff. You really don't need to worry about witches and werewolves." But what *was* the important stuff? I wanted to teach her about the world, but there was so much she didn't know. Where did I even start?

"What do you *want* to know?" I asked her.

Her eyelids flickered, the question just as big for her as it was for me. "Those clothes you were wearing when you arrived... are those... normal?" She wrinkled her nose a little at the idea.

I laughed. "Yes, and no. Jeans – those blue pants – are pretty common, but people wear all sorts of things. It's like... a way to express yourself, I guess."

She plucked at the sweater I'd given her, running her hand over it. "This is soft. And itchy."

I laughed again. "You've pretty much summed up sweaters."

She smiled too, but I'm not sure she fully got the joke. "I like watching people arrive. The little glimpses of outside they bring." She met my eye, then looked away quickly as if embarrassed. "We make up stories about them in the dorms. Try to imagine who they were before. You probably think that's silly."

I shook my head. "No, I used to do that too. People watching."

"But don't you know what their lives are like?"

"Not strangers, no."

"But..." She frowned, seeming to grapple with something, unable to grasp what I was saying. "Don't you all live together?"

It took me a moment to understand. She had no idea how big the outside really was. She thought everyone lived together and all knew each other, just like they did here.

"No," I said. "It's *really* big out there. I see hundreds – maybe thousands – of people I don't know, every day."

"That sounds scary."

I shrugged. "Sometimes. Sometimes it's nice."

We were quiet for a moment, staring up at the moon and the stars. So many more stars than I was used to. I'd had no idea how much of that was lost in the city.

"So... what story did you make up about me?" I asked.

She let out a half-laugh. "It was Alara's turn to make one up. She said that you and the man you were with both wore those matching blue pants because you were best friends, and you always wanted to be the same. She said you looked grumpy, because your friend had told you that you wouldn't be able to wear them anymore, and that you would each wear different colours here."

I chuckled at the story. I'd never thought about the fact that Dad's and my jeans were the same. I hadn't wanted to copy him since I was a little kid.

"Alara's stories are always about the clothes. She's not very imaginative." A flicker of something crossed Aria's face, and her mood fell. "She didn't get any further than that because we got caught. We're not supposed to talk about the outside world. Alara got taken to the repercussion rooms."

My own laughter died in my throat. "The repercussion rooms?"

Aria's body tensed beside me. "It's where they take you if you break the rules. They're out in the forest somewhere. I don't know exactly. They make you wear a bag over your head when they walk you out there."

Suddenly, I remembered the scream I'd heard my first night here, and the trail of figures walking out into the trees. Shamefully, I had almost accepted Mother's explanation that it had been a nightmare.

Aria sat up, hugging her knees to her chest. "The rooms are awful. It's always dark and cold out there, and the ceiling's so low you have to kneel."

"And they send you there every time you break a rule?" It sounded like torture. The thought of trapping kids in a place like that made me want to vomit.

Aria nodded. "The young people, at least. The adults have different consequences. I don't know what." She didn't meet my eye, and I had a feeling she had heard rumours, even if she didn't know for sure what the adult consequences entailed. I didn't press it, not wanting to make her talk about it.

"So why do you risk coming out here?" I asked instead. "If you know they might punish you like that?"

Her eyes shot up to meet mine. There was so much sadness in them, so much longing. "Because I can't stay trapped in here. Even if I get a consequence, I can't..." She trailed off, unable to articulate her desire for more than this sheltered life.

The real world was cruel sometimes. What happened to my family was proof of that. But at least there were choices. At least I could live an actual life out there, instead of whatever this was.

"If I find a way out, will you come with me?"

I didn't plan to say it, but after hearing about the repercussion rooms, there was no way I could leave her behind.

Aria barely took a breath before answering. "Yes."

The air seemed to go very still between us. This had to be huge for her. Had she thought about leaving before? Would her parents let her go on her own? If they objected, would she still want to come with me? I didn't know how I felt about influencing her decision. Then again, perhaps I was just the first person to offer her any semblance of a way out.

"Then, I will take you with me," I said. I hoped it was a promise I could keep.

WE STAYED OUT MOST of the night, talking until the sky began to lighten. I wouldn't have thought our senses of humour would be compatible, given our different upbringing, but twice Aria's stories of things the kids got up to behind Mother's back had me silently shaking with laughter, pressing my fists against my mouth to keep from making too much noise.

As for her, she just wanted to know everything I could tell her about the outside world. I'd never felt so interesting. She listened with rapt focus to me explaining things like swimming pools and non-pureed food. Honestly, sometimes it was like trying to translate to another language. How did you explain a motorway to someone who'd never even seen a car?

"We need to get back," she said finally. Her shoulders sank at the words, and I felt mine do the same.

"Yeah, we do." I pulled myself up, then reached out a hand to help her to her feet.

She didn't let go of it once she was standing. I liked the feeling of her fingers linking through mine, but more than that, I liked that this way I wouldn't get lost in the dark. I'd made this trip a few times now, but I still had the feeling I might take a wrong turn and disappear out there forever.

Aria had none of those fears. Her steps through the bush were easy, and she seemed to instinctively know when I was about to stumble. Her hand tightened on mine more than once, offering me a way to balance.

Suddenly, she stopped walking, her whole body going tense. Her grip on my hand turned from a hold to a crush.

"What is it?" I murmured, my voice only just audible.

She gave a slight shake of her head. The rest of her remained frozen.

I strained my eyes and ears, searching for any sign of what had frightened her. And then I heard it. The soft crunch of footsteps on the rough ground.

A line of muslin-clad figures appeared in the dark, moving towards us. If I hadn't known what they were, my mind would have strayed to the supernatural again. Their pale figures seemed to glow in the moonlight. They drifted through the trees, like old-fashioned depictions of ghosts in bedsheets.

I stepped backwards, dragging on Aria's hand. She didn't move. For a moment, I thought she knew something I didn't – something that would keep us safe by staying here. And then I saw the truth. She was shaking, rooted to the spot in terror.

"Come on," I hissed. "We have to move." I looped my arm around her waist, pulling her back.

She came with me this time, finally returning to her senses. I dragged her behind some bushes, and we crouched there, out of sight of the line of Retreaters. Were they taking someone out to the repercussion rooms? I hoped not. I didn't want any part in that after Aria's description.

"It's a consequence," Aria whispered, her voice high with panic.

I nodded. That much I had figured.

The figures formed a circle. It was only then that I noticed one of them had a bag over his head. They pushed him to the centre, then someone pulled the bag free.

"Please," the man said. "Please, I'm sorry!"

Aria started to shake again. I pulled her close to me, wrapping my arms around her. I didn't know what was about to happen, but I knew she shouldn't see it.

Something about the man was familiar. A tightness built in my chest, like my body knew the answer before I did. In my head, I saw his fist coming down on my face. The guy who punched me. This was my fault. He was here because of me.

None of the figures in the circle spoke. Instead, they each pulled something from inside their robes.

"Oh god." I pulled Aria closer to me, pressing her face into my chest and covering her ears with my hands.

Stones. They were each holding stones.

Bile rose in the back of my throat. "Don't look," I told her. "Whatever you do, don't look."

Something hit the man's leg, and I flinched. He let out a shout, scrambling back across the ground.

"Finn?" Aria whispered.

I looked down at her. Her eyes were so wide, and she shivered violently.

"Just don't move," I whispered. "Don't look."

I didn't see who had thrown it. I didn't know which one of them had been the first, but now all their hands were rising up.

Another stone hit him. Then another.

My fingers bit into Aria's shoulders, squeezing her too hard. I should help him. I should get off my ass and run in front of him. His eyes were wide, whites flashing in the moonlight. A stone hit his temple, and the noise he made was like that of an animal.

"Finn?" Aria said again.

Or maybe she didn't. Maybe I was just hearing her voice in my head, like Carly's and my mum's, all of them begging me to do something.

"Shh," I whispered. "Don't look."

His screams alternated with whimpers. How could they keep hitting him when he sounded like that? There was a soft, almost wet sound as each stone thudded into him, like a meat tenderiser hitting a piece of steak.

Aria squeezed her eyes shut. I didn't move. I didn't do anything to help him. I told myself I was protecting her. I told myself I couldn't get up without exposing her. But I knew deep down that I was just a coward.

"Please," the man yelled. "I'm sorry."

I closed my eyes and buried my face in Aria's hair. I couldn't face it anymore. But there was no way to block out the sound of his screams. Or the sound of those thuds.

NEITHER OF US MOVED for a long time after the figures left. The man was still whimpering as they carried him away. I didn't know how to feel about that. It meant he was hurt badly, but it also meant he was alive. I was glad to have confirmation of that at least.

Had Aria known? Had she known this was what they did to adults who broke the rules here? It was sick. He was being punished for violence with worse violence. How could Mother not see how awful that was?

A heavy weight built in my chest again. He was being punished for violence against me; violence that I started when I kicked him in the stomach. This was my fault, yet again.

Eventually, Aria stirred. "We have to go back," she said. Her voice was hollow, and she didn't look at me.

I nodded. "Yeah."

We couldn't get caught. The thought of that group of people raising stones to throw at Aria was an image I just couldn't take.

She unfolded herself, rising up to stand. She reached out, taking my hand, but she still didn't look at me.

We walked back in silence, not a word spoken until we reached the fence.

"I will get a message to you, when I know how to get your phone," she said.

I blinked. "You mean... you're still willing to help me?"

Her eyes flicked up to mine. "I have to. We can't stay, if...." She swallowed, her face paling.

I reached out instinctively, touching her arm. She swayed against my hands as if about to pass out. Was this the first time she had seen violence? Was this the first time she had heard someone that afraid?

"We can't meet again until after." She opened her eyes, her gaze suddenly steady. "But I will help you. We have to leave."

You have to get out, Finn... Go get help.

My mum's words echoed in the night air, so similar to Aria's now. I couldn't help wondering if I was making as big a mistake now as I had then.

Chapter Ten

Webs of cracks spread across the glass in front of me. The seatbelt cut into my neck, pinning me to the headrest. I turned, stretching out for Joey's hand. I couldn't reach it. A single trickle of blood ran down her fingers, over the edge of her booster seat, onto the upholstery. She shrieked, a high repeating scream that stabbed through me.

Mum's breathing was fast. Too fast. Too shallow.

I turned to her. Her face was pale, and her eyes wide. "You have to get out. Go get help, Finn. You have to get out."

Mum's side of the car was completely caved in, the truck that hit us wedged up against her. Twisted pieces of metal stuck out around her like claws.

I fumbled until I heard the click of my seatbelt unlatching, then punched the remaining glass from my side window with my elbow.

I crawled from the car, leaving them inside.

ANNABELLE'S KNOCK WOKE me with a start. Images from the dream – from the accident that had killed Mum and Joey – still swirled in my head. On the edges of it was something else. Images of the stones hitting the man in the woods.

My fault again.

Annabelle opened the door, stepping inside. She smiled, but then it faltered. "Are you well, Finn?" she asked.

I ran a hand over my face, brushing away the cold sweat. "I am well," I said. I got up, nudging past her and making my way to the shower block before she could ask any more questions.

DESPITE MYSELF, I FELL into the routine of The Retreat. Or at least, my version of it. I woke early every morning, feeding and cleaning the kittens before the power came back on. Each day, I showered and shaved – no unsafe beards for me – then walked with Annabelle over to the dining hall, searching for Aria in the faces of the people we passed. I ate oatmeal and pureed fruit for breakfast, sitting between Mother and Angelina. It was still only adults in the dining hall, the children and teenagers were kept away from me. I had seen them in the grounds, though, allowed out from between the tall dormitory blocks. Perhaps Mother wasn't afraid I would infect them in the open air.

None of the kids came up to me, though, and I didn't approach them. I was keeping my side of my bargain with Mother, or at least most of it. Besides, Aria had said she would find me when it was time.

During the day, I helped pick vegetables and fruit, other Retreaters showing me how to tell when they were nearly ripe. I stole ice, and stole moments to sneak away and feed the kittens.

I hadn't seen my father since that first day, but my worry about him had died down to a low bubbling in the back of my mind. I'd spent the last year worrying about him. Maybe it was someone else's turn.

"You're doing well, Finn," Mother told me, on the third night after I'd snuck out with Aria.

"Hm?" I'd been thinking about the jug of milk, running low again now the kittens were getting bigger. Their mouths stretched open for more each time I fed them.

Mother smiled, resting her hand lightly on my forearm. "I said you're doing well."

Angelina gently squeezed my other shoulder. My stomach rolled at her touch, and I had to breathe deeply to stop the vegetable stew pouring back out onto my plate.

"So well," Angelina echoed.

Don't touch me! I wanted to scream.

"You're happier now, no?" Mother asked.

I hesitated. I was, but not for the reasons she thought. "Why do you all do that?" I asked, gesturing to their hands. "Touch each other like this, I mean."

Mother glanced down at her hand, as if she hadn't even registered it was still on my arm. She gave me another gentle squeeze, then let go. So did Angelina, thankfully.

"Most people out in the world are touch starved," she told me. "I think you were when you arrived. It's not healthy. It's not safe."

I let out a breath. Moments like this, it was hard to fault her. I had felt the craving for physical contact when I'd arrived. I had missed my mother's warm embrace, and my sister's inability to respect personal space, insisting on telling a story two inches from my face. And I had wanted my dad to hug me. I had wanted my dad to come back from wherever it was inside himself that he'd disappeared to.

I couldn't tell Mother any of that.

"Touch starved," I said instead. "I didn't know there was a term for it."

I WANDERED OUT INTO the grounds after dinner. A few people were working on the garden still, but most were walking together, chatting. A few adults played a game with the children, something that looked like a cross between tag and leapfrog. They didn't seem to stick to family groups here, all of the adults taking responsibility for the kids. The young ones ran to anyone they could when they needed comfort or food. It was nice, but strange.

I considered trying to steal more ice, but there wasn't much point. The kittens would finish the jug of milk tonight, most likely. It was all well and good Aria saying to tell her when I needed more, but I hadn't seen or heard from her since the night we'd seen them stone the man in the bush. It was starting to feel like a dream – *she* was starting to feel like a dream.

I stared at the setting sun, looking out at the hills bathed in streaks of orange and peach. Somewhere out there was the real world – cities, houses. It didn't seem possible when all I could see was trees, stretching out in every direction.

"Tonight."

I started, my eyes snapping back from the horizon to the figure suddenly in front of me – a girl. She was younger than me, maybe thirteen or fourteen, only coming up to my shoulder. She didn't look at me, staring down at the ground instead. She hunched slightly, as if to adjust her robes.

"Did you...?" I trailed off. Clearly, I had imagined her speaking.

"Tonight," she whispered again. "Wait outside the dining hall after lights out. Aria will come find you."

I let out a breath. "You're Aria's friend."

She gave a short, sharp jerk of her head. I caught sight of a long blonde braid under the folds of muslin. "Aria said not to give you my name, just in case. Tonight. Don't be late." She flicked her robes, finished adjusting them, then straightened up.

"More milk," I hissed, desperate to get the message across before she left. "The kittens are nearly out."

She'd already turned away, but her hooded head bobbed as she walked off. Message received on both sides. I closed my eyes, tension seeping out of me at the news of progress. Tonight. I could hold on until then.

I FED THE KITTENS LIBERALLY that night, no need to ration now I knew more milk was coming. I wondered at Aria's friend, though. She was so little, in both age and stature. I was seventeen, most likely only a few years older than her, but it was more than the number of orbits around the sun. Seventeen was a lot older than thirteen in experience and cunning, and I puzzled at why Aria had decided to trust her. Perhaps they were sisters? Perhaps there was no one else.

I sat poised, craving the clunk of the power turning off, and the heavy fall of dark straight after it. To think, on the first night it had caused me fear.

I shot up as soon as darkness hit, but then froze, straining for sounds of movement. Aria had assured me everyone went to sleep as soon as the lights went out, but that couldn't be possible. Where were the insomniacs? The night owls? The daydreamers, who liked to lie awake thinking in the twilight hours? Maybe the promise of safety cured them all.

I stretched my hands out in front of me for balance and forced my feet into steps. If Aria said it was okay for me to wander now, then wander I would.

I made my way quickly to the dining hall, scuttling like a mouse, tracing the edges of the buildings. The only dim light came from the kitchen block outside the gate, casting a stretched, shadow version of the fence across the ground. I found my way half by touch and muscle memory, half by starlight. Smell aided me too, the dining hall still holding the scent of tonight's vegetable and lentil mush.

"Aria?" I whispered into the night.

"Here," the reply came, right behind me.

I jerked, spinning around, and then her hands were on my shoulders, her face and breath right next to mine.

"It's okay," she whispered. "It's me, Finn. It's me."

I relaxed into her touch, letting her hold me for a second, and then she pulled her hands away. My skin tingled with the absence of her, and I couldn't help thinking there might be something to Mother's touch starvation.

"Come on. We won't have much time. Mother comes to my dormitory sometimes during the night."

Aria took my hand, then creaked open the dining hall door, leading me inside.

If I had thought the night was black outside, then inside was obsidian. Nothing, not even a hint of vision greeted me. My free hand splayed out automatically, expecting chairs and tables to sprout up in front of us. Already, I imagined the clattering thunks of them hitting the floor, and the running feet that would follow. Then I remembered – there were no chairs, and the tables were only a foot high, perfect to smash into knees and shins, causing one of us to let out a pained shriek which would give us away.

Aria gripped me tightly, pulling me in close to her side. "I know the way," she whispered, "but you must stay close, or you'll hit something."

She moved easily in the dark, her gait even and soft beside my stumbling one. She slipped her arm around my waist, steadying me. I flinched, her hand tickling my side.

"Trust me," she whispered, her voice seeming to come from nowhere and everywhere.

"Okay. I do," I whispered back, ignoring the slight hitch in my voice.

She led me on a jagged path across the room, skirting tables. I began to feel them in the dark, the skin on my shins tingling like the tiny hairs were stretching out, responding to what I couldn't see. Spidey senses, or some new peripheral awareness power let my steps even out, trusting myself not to fall.

"Only a little further," she whispered, pulling me closer to her as we moved around another table. She stopped, then released her grip on me.

I clung to her robe, panic crawling its way up my throat. "Where are you going?"

She took my hand, freeing her clothes from its grasp. "It will be quicker if I go alone. Stay here." And she was gone.

It wasn't just the total darkness of the room that unnerved me, it was the silence. I swayed slightly on the spot, trying to find any frame of reference for the position of my body in space, but there was nothing. My limbs felt like they were growing; my head suddenly seemed very far away from my feet. Any special senses I'd gained were not only gone, they'd taken the regular ones with them.

"Here." Aria was suddenly beside me again, pressing something cold and hard into my hand. A key. A little click sounded, and she lit up with a soft green glow.

"What...?" I trailed off, the answer to my question becoming clear. Aria held a torch under her robes, using the fabric to muffle the light.

"Mother keeps this and the spare key in a hidden panel under her cushion in the dining room." Aria clicked the torch off, and disappeared into darkness. "I think it's in case the power goes out when we're in here. I'm not supposed to know the panel is there."

"Can't we leave it on?" Already, the blackness was pressing against me, and I reached hungrily for Aria's hand.

"No, it's too risky, and I don't know how long the baby light lasts. You'll need it once you're in Mother's cupboard."

Mother's cupboard – that sounded like something from a fairy tale, but I had a feeling this would be anything but. "Baby light?" I asked, then I clicked. "It's called a torch," I told her.

"Okay, whatever," she said, for once not eager for new words. "Come on, we don't have time." She slipped her arm around me again, leading me... somewhere. My sense of direction was not strong enough to navigate with so little stimulation. She edged us towards a wall, and ran her hand and my arm along it, just like my mouse-crawl around the buildings.

She stopped once again. "We're outside Mother's office. You'll have to go in alone," she told me. "The cupboard's not big enough for both of us, and I should stay and keep watch."

"I can't find my way alone."

"You can." Aria pressed the torch into my hands. "There's a window; it won't be as dark in there, and you can turn the torch on once you're inside the cupboard."

Her voice was so certain, so strong and full of belief in me. Even growing up in this place, being controlled and lied to, she'd found some way to grow that sense of self, to find a way within her own mind to fight.

I closed my fingers around the torch. "Okay. How do I find it?"

She took my shoulders in her hands again, this time moving to stand behind me. "The door is right in front of you, the doorknob halfway up. You'll have to remember to relock it if we get separated."

My stomach sank through my knees at that thought, but I nodded. Her lips were right behind my ear, her words whispered, breathy on my neck.

"When you get inside, turn left." She turned me as she said it, marking the directions with our bodies. "About three paces, and you'll hit the wall. Turn right—" again she physically turned me, "—and then about another four paces and you'll find the cupboard door. It's the same lock as the main door... I think."

"You think?" I turned my head, practically catching her lips with mine.

"I don't know. I've never managed to get in there before, but I think I've seen her open it with the same key. It looks the same, at least."

I sighed. She wouldn't know enough to realise that most keys came from similar blanks. They all looked the same at a distance. Yet, this was the only plan we had.

"We can only try," I told her.

"Yeah," she said softly. "Three paces, then four," she reminded me. "Close the cupboard door behind you before you turn the light on. If anyone's coming, I'll knock twice on the wall. If I knock three times, it means I have to run, and you're on your own."

I nodded, though she wouldn't be able to see it. All this for kittens.

"Can I see you tomorrow?" I asked. "If I don't see you again tonight."

There was silence for a moment, then her voice dropped even lower. "Tomorrow. Straight after lights out. At the river."

"I'll be there." Unless I got caught and withdrawn. With some effort, I pulled away from her. I ran my hand down the side of the door, finding the handle.

"The keyhole is on the handle," Aria whispered, but I'd already found it. Though it had never been this black, Carly and I had snuck out in the dark a few times. I slipped the key into the lock and turned it.

Click.

"Good luck," she whispered.

"You too."

I pulled the key from the lock and stepped inside before I could change my mind. Aria closed the door behind me, and my lungs squeezed, pressed flat by the dark. But Aria was right. In seconds, my pupils were taking in the meagre light from the window, straining to pick out shapes of furniture within the room. But there was no furniture, I reminded myself. Only hessian mats. I stretched out a toe, finding the coarse edge of one of them. Somehow that helped. I didn't want to go kneeling on it, especially not in front of Mother, but having the point of reference helped. I could picture the space now, sense its edges, rather than the endless expanse of inky shadow.

Okay. I turned left, took two and a half shaky paces, and smacked straight into the wall. "Ow," I said, though it was more out of surprise than pain. *Note to self, Aria's steps are shorter than mine.*

I turned, right this time, and took a couple of steps. She'd said four, but I guessed that was about three of mine. I didn't want to miss the cupboard door and spend the next hour fumbling around searching. I placed my fingertips on the wall, letting them trail as I took the next step. There it was. The tiniest of bumps under my hand, and the texture of the wall changed from paint to rough wood.

My hand tightened around the key. *Find the doorhandle, Finn. Don't panic, just find the handle.* I traced across to the righthand side of the door, running my palm up and down it. No handle.

"Shit," I whispered. Was it like the hidden panel Aria had said was under Mother's cushion? Would I have to knock the correct number of times, or press the exact right spot? But no... Aria had said she'd seen Mother use a key.

I ran my hand over the wood again, slower this time. A keyhole, maybe, not a handle. Easy to miss when rushing. I forced myself to brush the wood slowly, methodically covering the length of it, then inching my fingers back and beginning again, tracing down a spot slightly to the left.

My fingers hit something cold and round; a small metal bump. *Yes...* I kept my hand on it, bringing the key up to meet it. I traced the ridges of the key, then the sliver-sized gap where it was to be inserted. Which way up? I'd have to try it one way and hope it didn't get stuck if I was wrong.

Three frustrating tries, and the key slid into the lock. I let out a breath, and turned the key. The door opened, and I stepped inside.

The space was tight, I didn't need Aria or to touch the sides to tell me that. The pressure of the narrow walls bore down on me. The air inside felt thick, hot, as if it was trying to push me back.

Not for you, it seemed to say. *Stay back.*

I moved further inside anyway, closing the door behind me and turning on the torch.

The space was even tighter than I had imagined. The roof of the cupboard brushed the sticking-up strands of my wayward hair. I could reach my hands out on either side of me, though, and I did so now, reassuring myself that I could move. What was with this place? I'd never been afraid of the dark, nor considered myself claustrophobic, but now I was fearing both night and tight spaces.

"Get it together, Finn," I said to myself.

I had to. There wasn't time for me to freak out.

I scanned the small room. This wasn't what I was expecting. Rather than an organised storage space, or even a disorganised one, this was more like some type of shrine. Old photographs and children's drawings lined the walls. Pain built in my throat, and heat pricked behind my eyes. These could have been Joey's drawings.

I pulled one of the photos gently from the wall. In it, a younger version of Mother smiled down at a baby in her arms. She wore a green dress, and the baby was wrapped in a pale green blanket. The son she had lost.

The back of the photo moved, springing out. It had been folded in half before being pinned to the wall, but I didn't straighten it out. The last thing I needed was to leave evidence I'd been in here by damaging it. I pinned it back up instead and turned away.

At the back of the cupboard, several plastic tubs were stacked against the wall, with a few smaller cardboard boxes piled on top. This was more like it. I aimed the torch in their direction, refusing to let myself look at any more of the photos.

I carefully took the boxes down, trying to remember where each one went. One of the tubs was labelled "ready for sale". Well, I guess that explained where this place got the money to keep running. Selling people's belongings when they arrived would be a good little income stream. I had a horrible feeling it wasn't their only source of income, though. I'd overheard several terse phone calls between Dad and the bank before we left home. I suspected signing over your worldly assets was a condition of coming here.

I opened one of the other tubs and peered into it. Miscellaneous papers and books; no sign of anything technological. I lifted it down and opened the one underneath.

Bingo.

My heart lifted at seeing a phone charger cable spring out from under the lid, an adaptor still attached to the end. Then my guts plummeted all the way back down, taking my heart with them. The tub was full, and I mean *full*, of phones, laptops and other electronics. Identical, black, shiny phones. Finding mine in here was going to take time I did not have.

"Think, Finn. Breathe."

It was my mum's voice not mine that seemed to cross my lips. *Think it through. What do you know?* she used to say.

What did I know?

I knew that Dad and I were the most recent arrivals, so our phones should be near the top. That was something. I took a breath. It came a little easier now my insides were returning to their proper places. I knew that neither Dad nor I could afford an iPhone, so I could discount all the ones with a half-bitten apple on the back. I knew that three weeks before Dad shoved our lives into the back of a car, Carly had dropped my phone. I'd been fighting to get it back from her, as she threatened to go into my messages and tell some girl I had a crush on her. I couldn't remember which girl I'd liked that week, but I did remember the chip Carly's fumble had left on the top righthand corner of my phone.

There it was. A phone with a chip. "Bless your clumsy hands, Carly," I whispered into the dark.

I pulled the phone out and went to press the power button.

I stopped myself, thumb hovering. Would it have charge still? If it did, it had to be miniscule. Dare I turn it on? Would it be better to wait until I was back in my room, so I could actually use it?

I glanced at the box. Perhaps it would be better to grab a few phones. Some of them had to have charge. I didn't feel great about stealing, but it's not like their owners were using them...

Of course, only my phone had Carly's phone number. "Dammit!" I nearly threw it across the ridiculously tiny cupboard.

I stopped, forcing myself to breathe. I had a charger.

I flashed the torch around the cupboard, on the off chance there was a power socket. When was the last time I had seen one? Given I didn't have anything to plug in, I hadn't exactly been looking. Even so, I suspected they were like light switches here: non-existent. But if there was going to be one anywhere, this would be the place.

Down near the floor I found one. I crouched, shoving the adapter and charger into it, then the cable into the phone. I waited for a blue light to appear.

Nothing happened.

"Come on, come on..." I wiggled the charger, hoping it just wasn't plugged in properly. Then, reality ground into place. It wasn't the charger. The power was off.

"Stupid, stupid, stupid!" I pounded my fist against my forehead. All this work to get here, all the risk for Aria, and it was for nothing.

It couldn't be for nothing. *Think, Finn. Think.*

Knock, knock.

Shit.

Of course someone would come now. I started shoving everything I'd moved back into place. After a moment's indecision, I grabbed two more phones before closing the lid on the tub. I wanted to take all of them, but I had to play it safe. I couldn't take more, otherwise Mother might notice. Besides, the ones closest to the top had the most chance of still holding a charge.

I went to put the last cardboard box back when the writing on the side caught my eye. I turned it over, reading it properly. *No way.* It was a router box.

Knock, knock, knock.

Double shit.

I quickly opened the box, grabbing the documents from inside, before returning it empty to its original spot. I switched off the torch and bundled the stolen items into my robe, then readied the key in my hand. Outside the cupboard, I fumbled with the key, somehow finding the lock and turning it.

It was too late. I heard what Aria had heard – footsteps in the dark. I shrank back against the wall of Mother's office, clutching my stolen booty to my chest. I would be withdrawn for sure. Not for the first time, I let myself think about what that might mean. Would I be tossed out into the wilderness, left to trek my own way home? Would they at least let me call someone to come get me?

The footsteps paused in the corridor, and a soft light crept under the door. I didn't dare breathe. *I'm not here,* I said inside my head. *I'm invisible.* I willed it to be true. I willed myself not to exist anymore. It wasn't just my future on the line, it was

Aria's. I'd never tell where I got the torch or the key from, but someone would find out. Someone always found out.

The footsteps started again, slower, moving away. I held my breath still, though it burned in my chest. I held it until my head pounded and I could feel my pulse in my ears. Finally... finally... there was silence. I exhaled, the air exploding from me, then I held my breath once more, listening. There was nothing. No footsteps, no sounds.

I was safe. I was safe, and I had three phones with just the slimmest possibility that at least one of them still held a charge.

Chapter Eleven

I didn't dare risk going back into the cupboard. I doubted there was anything else in there that could help me, even if it was tempting to keep searching in the tiny sliver of hope that there might be. I had the phones; that was enough.

I hoped Aria had made it to her own room without getting caught. Now, it was my job to get myself back to my own room before I gave her away.

I found the outer doorhandle of Mother's office, and locked it behind me, remembering Aria's caution. Of course, we had forgotten one important part of the exit strategy if we were separated. I did not know the way in the dark.

I stood for a moment, the night pressing helplessness into my every pore. I still had the torch, but light was a risk I wasn't willing to take.

Outside, I had found my way by hugging the edges of the buildings, like a rodent on an illicit scavenging journey. Indoors, I could take that one step further. I dropped to my hands and knees, crawling along the corridor.

I don't know how long it took – the painstaking three-limbed crawl, as I clutched my phone and other stolen treasures to my chest. I knew when I reached the dining hall, only because the floor surface changed from wooden floorboards to some type of lino, but I don't know how long it took me to cross it. Far longer than it had taken with Aria's confident steps across the middle of the room. I hit three corners before I found the door, going the long way around, only realising when it was too late for it to make sense to turn back. Finally, I found it. My shoulder bumped the wooden door frame, and I reached up in relief at finding a way out. Of the dining room, that was. I was still trapped in The Retreat's box.

Patches of grey painted the sky outside, signs of the coming dawn. I raced to my room, barely bothering to stay hidden this time. I scrambled inside and closed my door behind me, leaning back against it and sucking air into my lungs.

But no – there was no time to waste. I fumbled with the torch and the key, finding the end of the charger before my phone.

I pressed the phone's power button to light it up. Four percent power. Only four bloody percent. But there was a worse problem, and nausea rolled through me at seeing it. There was no signal. Of course there was no signal; we were in the middle of nowhere. How stupid had I been to go through all this, just to be left with a phone I couldn't even use?

No. Don't give up yet. I forced myself to breathe. To think.

I grabbed the papers I'd taken from the router box, flipping through them. It was a long shot, but maybe, I thought... just maybe...

There it was. The little sticky-backed note you're supposed to attach to the bottom of the router. The one with the default network name and password.

I typed the details into the Notes app on my phone, then clicked through to settings, finding my way to the Wi-Fi options. The circle of doom revolved on my screen. Mother seemed the type to worry about everything from the impacts of social media to electromagnetic radiation, but she had to have some way of contacting the outside world. She didn't seem like she'd be the most technologically adept. Was it too much to hope she hadn't bothered to change the default settings? After all, she didn't have to protect the network, when no one else had a device.

The circle on my screen was still spinning. Either she had hidden the network somewhere, or I was too far away. I cursed myself for not trying to connect while I was still in Mother's office.

But no. The router would need power. I was pretty sure the only place where I'd find that was the kitchen building on the other side of the fence.

It took everything in me not to sprint across the grounds to the gate. Instead, I crept outside, glancing at my phone every few feet. And then there it was. An available network with the same generic string of letters and numbers as I'd seen on the sticker.

I copied and pasted in the password as quickly as I could. My thumb hovered over the connect button for a moment; prayers or wishes or whatever you want to call them filled my head. *Please say she never changed it...*

I clicked the button. And it connected.

I let my head drop back, eyes to the sky in relief, but only for a moment. There was no time to lose. I had three percent power. Just getting connected had wasted a whole precious percent!

I ignored the hundreds of emails and other notifications that popped up, going straight to my messaging app. I clicked on Carly's name. Then stopped. What could I say? And where even was I? I shook my head.

There was only one way to do this, but it would drain the battery. First, I needed a backup plan.

I switched apps, opening my barely used phone contacts, and scrolled to Carly's name once again. I found the number and repeated it aloud. I whispered it to myself again and again, desperately trying to commit the digits to memory. The numbers seemed to jumble and rearrange themselves, but I had to get it right.

I swallowed. "Here goes nothing."

I switched back to the messaging app. I quickly typed out "SMN". Save Me Now. Carly's and my version of an SOS.

Then I opened up maps, knowing that the GPS signal would almost immediately drain the battery. I dropped Carly a pin of my location. The word "sending..." appeared and with it another circle of doom.

It was too much to ask – sending her a location in the middle of nowhere, expecting her to get in her car and drive for days to find me. I also knew she would do it.

The screen went black.

My fingers tightened around the phone, as if I could squeeze power back into it. Had it sent? Please god, had it sent?

I fumbled with the other phones I'd stolen, pressing down hard on their power buttons. No beeps. No lights. Nothing. They were both dead as dead.

That was it. My one chance at rescue done. And I had no way of knowing if it had worked.

BY THE MORNING, IT felt like a dream. The dead phones and the stolen key were solid reminders that our midnight journey had happened, but had I really got the message off to Carly? Was it possible she was on her way now? My mind tore between clawing hope that she was, and horror at what I had asked her to do. I needed to talk to her – give her more instructions. She couldn't just rock up here. That would only result in her being dragged inside, indoctrinated and shoved into a muslin robe.

I searched every inch of the room for a power point, just in case, but I already knew there wouldn't be one. After all, I wasn't supposed to have anything that could be plugged in.

Finally satisfied – or rather dissatisfied – that there were no outlets, I fed the kittens. They all tugged at my fingers when it was their turn, and those in the box clambered over each other trying to reach me. Or just to escape, I couldn't tell. They'd chewed the edges of the box, leaving soggy cardboard lined with vicious teeth marks. It wouldn't hold them for much longer.

I thought about taking the key and torch with me over to the dining room, somehow sneaking them back into the panel under Mother's cushion. The logistics of getting the keys under Mother's seat while she sat upon it eating breakfast defeated me.

I slipped my phone into the pocket of my boxers instead. It was useless without power but having it close by was familiar – comforting. Sort of. I debated taking the charger too, just in case there was an accessible power point somewhere along the way, but the bulge it made under my robe was bound to give me away. Not to mention the improbability of getting uninterrupted charging time, with so many people around.

If I found a suitable power point, I'd sneak back and get the charger. That was the sensible way to do it. In the meantime, it could live in the cupboard with the kittens. I hid the keys under my mattress, along with Dad's and my stolen clothes.

Dad.

When had I last thought about him, let alone seen him? I shook my head. It didn't matter. If all went to plan, he and I would be driving home with Carly very soon.

"Are you well, Finn? Did you sleep safely?" Annabelle asked me, on the way to the dining hall.

I couldn't help scanning the ground and corners of the room for signs of disruption – signs that I'd slipped up and damaged something or left traces of my disobedience behind. Nothing caught my eye, and I let myself relax just a little.

"I am well," I told her. I turned towards her as I said it, and something made me pause. "Are you?" The pallor of her skin suggested she wasn't. Her lips were pale, and the corners of her mouth tightly drawn.

"I am safe," she told me. "Everything is well here." She smiled, but it didn't reach her eyes.

"Okay..." I wanted to tell her to talk to a doctor, but were there even doctors here? There was the health room, but I couldn't help thinking the treatments were probably much further along the woo woo spectrum than I would be comfortable with. The nearest hospital must have been miles away, and it would have taken hours for an ambulance to arrive.

Why was I thinking of that? Annabelle didn't need an ambulance. She was just a little pale.

She touched my arm. "I'm fine, Finn. I promise." She gently pushed me away, towards Mother's table.

"Okay, but... you let me know if you need anything, yeah?"

Annabelle's eyes crinkled at that, and she nodded. "I will. Thank you." She turned away, and I made my way up to the raised platform where Mother and Angelina stood, the cushion between them waiting for me. Neither of them sat down. Another woman stood beside them, Mother's hand on her shoulder.

Mother smiled as I reached her, but her attention soon turned to the rest of the room. "Today, we have an exciting announcement to make." Mother drew the woman beside her forward. "Amelia is going to bring a baby to The Retreat."

Amelia beamed, her hand pressed lightly to her stomach. Even through the folds of fabric, I could see her belly lay flat underneath it. So, The Retreat wasn't opposed to pregnancy tests.

"I ask you all to join me in wishing Amelia farewell and blessing her with safety."

"Farewell, Amelia," the room chanted. "We bless you with safety."

Angelina slipped her arm through Amelia's, and together they walked through the room. As she passed each table, hands stretched out to touch her, the blessing repeated in murmurs.

Mother sat down. The floor underneath her cushion creaked. My eyes flicked downward, to the panel hidden underneath. I forced my gaze back up. Would she be able to tell

Aria had been in there? How often did she check her emergency supplies?

"Where is Amelia going?" I asked Mother, hoping to distract her. A more important question about Amelia might have been, "Why the hell is that callous excuse for a human being, Angelina, going with her?"

Annabelle touched Amelia's arm as Amelia and Angelina passed her, and tears on Annabelle's cheeks caught the light. Happy or sad tears?

I frowned. Annabelle wasn't okay, I was sure of it.

"Amelia will spend her pregnancy in the care of the health team," Mother told me. "It is a dangerous time, and we must keep her safe."

I couldn't deny this was true – Mum had spent most of her pregnancy with Joey throwing up, until her face turned thin and dark circles lined her eyes, and still her belly kept growing. I had a feeling there might be more to it, though. Aria had been baffled by the sudden appearance of the kittens, with no understanding of where they had come from. Mother was taking Amelia away, not just to keep her safe, but to protect her careful sheltering of the children here.

"I understand," I told her. She smiled at me, not hearing the other meaning behind my words.

I ESCAPED THE DINING hall as soon as I could. The other Retreaters had rejoiced at the news, excitement bubbling through the enforced post-meal conversation. I couldn't join it. What kind of life was it for a baby born into this? The one good thing had been that Angelina didn't return. My mushy food went down a lot easier without her beside me.

I sat down next to the vegetable patch and pulled up carrots, placing them in a basket beside me. The work was boring, but my mind was on counting down the hours until lights out, when I would see Aria again.

"Did you get it?"

The voice beside me startled me, but I knew enough not to turn around. I tilted my head slightly, catching sight of Aria's blonde-braided friend. She used a small brush to pollinate tomatoes in the patch beside me.

"I did," I said quietly. "I sent a message to my friend." At least I hoped I had. "I'll need to contact her again, though."

The girl made a soft sound between her lips. "Can you send her another text?"

I blinked at the question. If this girl knew about texts, then she couldn't have grown up here. That explained why she was allowed to spend time in the yard with me, when the others weren't. Perhaps that's why Aria had chosen her to help too.

"No, there's no signal, and I'm out of battery. I've got a charger, but I can't find an outlet anywhere."

The girl made a noise in her throat. "Good luck with that. There's like two, and they're in the common areas and have stuff plugged into them."

The common areas where there were people all the time. Great. "Is there anyone here who might have a phone? I know Carly's number, if we can just find a way to call it." At least, I hoped I knew it. I'd chanted the number over and over in the dark last night, until I fell asleep, but as my teachers would tell you, memory has never been my strong suit.

"There's a landline in the office. Talk to Aria. She'll figure out a way to get you back in, I'm sure."

Did landlines need power, though? It had been years since we'd had one at home, but I seemed to remember it just having the one cable, no power cord.

"Can you get a message to Aria?" I asked.

The girl shook her head. "Maybe. I'm not sure. I'm not supposed to talk to her either."

That figured, especially if I was right and she'd been born outside The Retreat.

"But if I can't," she continued, "she'll meet you tonight as planned. Leave the torch and key under your mattress."

I nodded. "Already there."

"Perfect. One of us will get them."

"How many of you are there?"

The girl didn't answer, and when I turned to look, she was gone.

I WASN'T TRYING TO keep watch, but all day my eyes strayed back to the door to my room, looking for anyone going in or out. I never saw anyone, but when I next checked under my mattress, the torch and key were gone.

One of the knots in my stomach unravelled at that. It tightened right back up again at the thought of Aria or the blonde girl being caught with them. The sooner I could get us all out of here, the better.

Only a few more hours of gardening, and mushy food eaten next to Mother, until I could see Aria again, I told myself. And hopefully, only a few more days until Carly would come.

Chapter Twelve

"Finn?"

My name in Aria's voice was like music in the night. "Here," I called back, as loudly as I dared. Her hand found mine, and squeezed it, not so cold this time.

"Come on," she whispered. "Let's go sit by the river."

We made our way along the bank, until we came to the fallen log where we could sit without getting our robes muddy or wet. I'd brought clothes again. A jacket for her, and a sweater for me. She pulled her arms into the sleeves eagerly, her shivers increasing at the prospect of warmth.

"You can do it up with the... you know what? I'll just do it." I pulled the zip up for her. She stared, fascinated as the moonlight glinted against the metal teeth, and she trailed her hand over mine as I zipped her up.

"There," I said. "Nice and warm." Just like Mum used to say to me when I was still learning how to do my own fastenings. I sat back, but Aria shuffled closer to me.

"No, stay close. I'm still cold."

I grinned, and moved in right beside her, putting my arm around her shoulder. With any other girl, this might have been a come on, but this was Aria, the girl who had stripped naked in front of me, and who had never had the birds and bees talk. I shook my head. I could keep her warm without it being anything else.

"You got a message to your friend?" she asked.

I nodded. "Yeah, I think so. But I need to talk to her, if I can."

"Ada said there's something in the office you can use."

Ada – so that was the blonde girl's name. I didn't acknowledge Aria's slip, and she didn't seem to realise she'd accidentally spoken her co-conspirator's name.

"Do you think your friend is already coming, though?" Aria asked.

"I think so." Carly and I had only ever used SMN for the worst of emergencies, and I'd never abused that. She would know it was important and do everything she could to come. "It just depends on whether she can leave without her mothers knowing."

Aria jerked slightly, then stiffened. "Mothers? There's another one?"

"No, not that kind of Mother. Her mothers. Her mums."

Aria turned to look at me. The moon hung only slightly less than full above us, the light giving me an impression of her face. She stared at me. Her brows dropped into a frown, and her eyes flicked back and forth between mine as if searching for an answer there.

I felt my expression mirror hers. "You have a mum, don't you? Or a dad?"

She shook her head slowly. "We just have Mother."

"But..." A curdling nausea swirled in my stomach. "You do know what parents are, don't you?"

She shook her head, and anything else I'd been going to say dissolved in a puff of air. That morning, Mother had said Amelia would be bringing a baby to The Retreat. I hadn't realised she meant that literally – that Amelia might not get to raise the baby, to claim it as her own. No wonder all the kids I'd seen ran to any adult nearby instead of looking for their own mum or dad.

"How long have you lived here?" I asked her.

She shrugged. "Always."

"And in all that time, you've never seen anyone with parents?" A need to hug my dad crept over me. The feeling was so strong, it was like his body was a missing part of mine. I hadn't hugged him in years, but I wanted to wrap my arms around him now. Would I even see him again? Would The Retreat keep us separated forever?

Aria shook her head. "What are they? Par-ents?" She pronounced the word carefully, another one for her growing glossary.

It wasn't a concept I'd ever had to explain. "So, out in the real world... my world," I corrected. I wasn't sure she'd take too kindly to the implication that her world was imaginary. "People don't live in big groups like this. They live in families, usually."

She didn't answer, the frown still set in place.

I sighed. "So, kids, they normally live with their mum and dad... or two mums," I added, thinking of Carly. "Or two dads, or maybe only one of either. Their parents, at least, whatever combination they have." But then there were families where the grandparents raised the kids, or aunts and uncles. "The point is, they're all related." Except, no, there were families which weren't related by blood too. The more I thought about it, the harder I found it to explain the concept of "family". I just knew it when I saw it.

"Sounds complicated," Aria said.

I laughed. "It's not, I swear, it's just..." I turned my head towards her just as she turned her face towards mine. "It's wonderful," I said softly. "It's full of warmth and love. At least, that's what it's supposed to be."

Something crossed Aria's face – sadness, and longing for things she didn't understand. "That's what it's supposed to be here, too."

Supposed to be, but it wasn't. For all their talk of safety, I'd never felt more afraid. I suspected many of the people here had never felt more lonely.

Aria looked up at me, meeting my eye. "Can we be a family? You and me?"

"I..." A lump formed in my throat. A found family. My biological one was gone, but it didn't mean I couldn't build another.

Aria's face fell at my silence. "I'm sorry. Did I say the wrong thing?"

"No. Not at all." I touched her shoulders, holding them just like Mother did to mine. The irony of that wasn't lost on me, but in that moment, the gesture felt right.

She reached up, gently cupping my face and running a finger under my eye. "But you're crying," she said.

I hadn't realised that I was until that moment. "It's okay," I said. "It's not a bad thing."

She smiled hesitantly and leaned in closer to me.

I kissed her.

I didn't mean to, but her lips were right there, moving towards mine. She tasted like the air here, fresh and with just a hint of pine needles.

Shit. What was I doing? She was so innocent, so naïve, and this was some predatory bullshit from me.

I pulled back. "I'm sorry. I shouldn't have... I'm sorry."

"It's okay," she whispered.

But it wasn't. "I'm sorry," I said again. "I should go." I stood up, backing away.

"Finn, wait," she called after me, but I didn't stop.

MY HEAD SWUNG THE NEXT day. One moment reliving the soft press of Aria's lips as she kissed me back. The next cringing at the memory, cursing my lack of self-control. I'd messed everything up. Without Aria's help I'd never get to the phone to call Carly. Without her, I'd never get back to my dad, or my life. Without Aria... without Aria, I would be without Aria.

"Your jacket's back under your bed."

I looked up at the sound of the voice. I hadn't bothered with the pretence of picking vegetables today, instead sitting on the stairs, blankly staring out at the fence and the thick of trees beyond it.

Ada sat behind me, a few steps up, and a few paces to the left. "You could have really screwed her over, leaving her with it."

"Shit. I didn't even think about that."

"Don't swear. It's like a dog whistle to Mother." Ada's tone held the certainty of experience. She'd been like me, once – new and forced to acclimate to this strange, controlled world.

"Your name's not really Ada, is it?" I wasn't even supposed to know that moniker, but suddenly this felt important.

She didn't answer, and if I hadn't been able to see the end of her robe out of the corner of my eye, I would have questioned whether she'd walked away.

"My name is Finn Bryant," I said. "But it won't be for much longer, will it?"

"No," came the quiet reply. "They'll rename you once they think they've broken you."

Broken me. The acclimation process would get worse.

"How long have you been here?" I asked.

"Two years... I think. It's hard to tell time here." Her breath hitched a little. "I want out."

I nodded. "Me too."

She practically snorted. "Then what was last night? You ran off and left her without making a proper plan." Her voice rose, and heads turned our way. I leaned forward, picking up something imaginary from by my feet. My cheeks flamed, and I let the folds of fabric fall over my face, hiding me. I felt her still, calming herself, then she took a breath.

"It was complicated," I told her, once I was sure the others had lost interest in us. "I did something I shouldn't have."

"You kissed Aria, big whoop." The girl kept her voice soft this time, but her derision came through clearly anyway. "You still shouldn't have run off."

I opened my mouth to speak, but then goldfished it as nothing came out. Aria had told Ada? Did that mean she wasn't horrified by what I'd done?

"She's not a child, Finn. The people here are weirdly isolated, but she's still a normal sixteen-year-old. She was happy you kissed her. I mean, she needed a bit of explaining, which was extremely awkward thank you very much, but she was happy. Well... at least, until you ran away."

Aria was happy. Relief and even more confusion filled me at that.

"So, don't screw this up, okay? Tonight, we'll get you back inside, you'll phone your friend, and you'll get us and those stupid kittens out, right? We're counting on you."

I could barely take in what she was saying, but I found myself nodding anyway. "Right."

"Good. Tonight. Outside the dining hall." She stood, walking down the stairs as if she would go straight past me. Then as she drew level with me, she stopped, stooping as if to fix her robe. "My name is Lucy Rogan. I'm thirteen years old... Maybe fourteen, depending on what the date is."

I nodded, taking all that in.

"Lucy Rogan," she repeated. "Remember that name, because I'm going to use it again soon."

Chapter Thirteen

Sneaking out had become easy – routine. I fed the kittens, then bundled them back in their box, ready for the clunk of darkness hitting. I took the phone and charger with me. The power would be off, but I thought perhaps I could plug my phone in inside the cupboard, then leave it to charge during the day. I'd have to pray Mother didn't find it, and that wasn't even the biggest risk. Getting it back would mean yet another midnight trip to retrieve it.

I traced the outsides of the buildings, my route familiar now even when I couldn't see it. I stopped outside the dining hall, my breath condensing in front of me in the cold air.

"Aria?" I breathed.

"Finn," came the answering call, and her hands found mine.

"Yeah, yeah, you're happy to see each other. Let's get inside." Ada – or rather, *Lucy* – bumped my shoulder, pushing between us.

I smiled at Aria, and I caught a glimpse of her teeth in the dark, smiling back. I could practically hear Lucy's eyeroll. And then we were all diving into the darkness.

"Do you need to go get the key?" I asked.

"No. I never put it back. She doesn't check it often," Aria whispered.

That seemed a risky game, to bet on Mother not choosing today to check the panel under her cushion, but *all* of this was a giant risk. Still, something niggled at the back of my mind, some warning. I couldn't quite put my finger on it.

"Then why do we need three of us?"

Lucy made a noise in her throat. "Just say if you don't want me here."

"I didn't mean—"

"I'm teasing you."

I frowned. Now was not exactly the time.

"We're going to try and get you more time, so you can make the call. Lookouts in both directions."

I nodded, but I wasn't sure how that would help. Warning me that someone was coming didn't magically make them disappear.

"Speaking of time... go on, attach yourself to Aria. We've got to get this thing moving."

I don't know how I'd seen Lucy as less worldly than me earlier. She was younger, yes, but she knew exactly what she was doing. She took the lead, stepping confidently out into the dark room in front of us, while I clutched Aria's hand, unable to cross the room unaided. Aria slipped her arm around my waist again, and with Lucy melting into the black it felt as if we were alone.

My breaths suddenly sounded very loud, and sweat seeped from my skin in the exact spot where her side pressed against mine. God, I hoped she couldn't feel it. She pushed me forward, and I stumbled over my own feet.

"Are you okay?"

I nodded, then breathed "yeah" when I remembered she couldn't see the movement of my head. I wanted to talk to her, to tell her I was sorry for kissing her... or to kiss her again, I wasn't sure which. With either option, I wanted it to happen at any other time than when we were walking through a pitch-black room to make a phone call that our futures depended on.

"Nearly there," Aria whispered, her face tantalisingly close to mine, her breath brushing my cheek.

"Okay," I whispered again.

She led me into the corridor. I couldn't see it of course, but I felt the change in the air around us, and in the surface beneath our feet. I was starting to understand how they did this – how they navigated through the night. Another two years, and I would be as good as them. I shuddered internally at the thought of still being here in two years' time.

"Here." Aria placed my hand on the doorknob of Mother's office. "I'm going to go to the end of the corridor to watch for signs of anyone coming. Ada will look after you."

Ada aka Lucy reappeared on the other side of me, touching my shoulder to let me know where she was.

"Aria, I..." I what? I needed to say something, but what? *I like you*, was what came to mind, but that seemed stupid and irrelevant right at this moment.

She squeezed my hand when I didn't continue. "I'll see you soon," she told me. She pulled her hand away, disappearing down the corridor.

"Ridiculous," Lucy muttered. I resisted the urge to tell her to shut up.

"Where is the landline?" Our plan rested on me being able to navigate the office and find the phone, which suddenly seemed like quite a big flaw.

"The right-hand corner of the room, last time I saw it."

I tried to picture that first day, when Dad and I arrived. I remembered the office, I remembered sitting on the hessian rug, I remembered Mother's creepy, benevolent-seeming smile, but I did not remember a landline. That didn't mean much. There'd been so much to take in, it hadn't exactly been my focus.

"When was that?"

I felt Lucy shrug. "A couple of months ago. Aria's been in there since then, but she doesn't know what she's looking for."

I scraped my free hand down my face. Me navigating my way in the office suddenly didn't seem like the biggest problem with this plan. "This is absurd."

Lucy nodded. "That it is, but so is this place."

I couldn't argue with that.

"You'll probably have to use the torch to dial but try not to risk it until you have to. And aim the beam away from the window. Aria and I will give you as long as we can." Lucy squeezed my shoulder, then let go.

I took a breath, then unlocked the door and slipped inside. I stood for a moment, trying to get my bearings. Last time, Aria's directions hadn't exactly been accurate, what with neither of us accounting for her shorter steps, but at least they had been something. I realised too late that I hadn't clarified whether she meant the righthand corner by the door or the one on the other side of the room by the window. And which direction was she facing when she said right?

I shook my head. *Don't overcomplicate this, Finn.*

I made my way along the wall to the first righthand corner. I'd check all four corners if I had to.

I reached the wall and dropped to the floor, searching. I didn't remember any tables in here, which meant it had to be on the floor. Nothing in this corner. I didn't let myself give in to the disappointment, following the wall to the second corner instead. I stayed low this time, checking the length of the skirting board for the phone or even a cable. My head bumped against the wall, signalling I'd hit the second corner. I patted the hessian floor mat in front of me, fingertips searching for anything electronic. Nothing.

"Dammit!"

Lucy must have been facing the other way when she'd said righthand side, or the phone had been moved since she'd last seen it.

Too many variables. Too little time.

I sighed, turning to make the crawl across the room to the other side. Then I stopped. I'd been thinking the phone had to be on the floor because there was no furniture, but what if it was attached to the wall itself?

I should have been checking everywhere. I'd wasted too much time already. Should I go back to that first corner? Retrace my steps and start again?

Stop. Breathe, came my mother's voice. *Think it through. What do you know?*

I scanned my memory of Mother's office one more time. The walls were a creamy colour... there'd been macramé wall hangings, and... yes! I remembered something solid and white in the back righthand corner.

I stood and ran my hand up the wall. The knuckle on my little finger connected with something. I moved my palms over it, finding buttons, a spiral cord, a receiver – an old-school phone, but still a phone. Finally!

"Hey!" My head snapped around at the shout from the corridor. There'd been no knock, no warning signal, but now there were running footsteps. And then a scream.

I bolted through the dark, towards where I thought the door was. By some miracle, I hit it. I yanked it open, but a sudden force shoved it back towards me.

"Ari—" I got half her name out before a hand slammed against my teeth.

"Shut up, just shut up!" Lucy hissed.

"But we need to—" My words muffled against her hand, and she squeezed tighter, cutting off my air.

"She knew she'd be caught. We both did. Now get back in there and make that call while I lead them away." She released her hand, and I stumbled backwards a pace.

"What?"

"It's the only way, Finn. You got caught for her, now she's doing it for you." Lucy disappeared into the dark, closing the door behind her.

"No! That's not the same thing!"

What we were doing now was worse than my stupid game with the wet robes, and Aria and Lucy were proper members of The Retreat, not just acclimating like me. Their punishments would be worse than mine. I could already hear Lucy's footsteps running away.

"You can't catch me," she sing-songed, in the same way I'd yelled as I ran to the bathrooms with the wet robe. Footsteps chased after her, drawing her pursuers away from me, and hopefully away from Aria.

I turned back to the window. I had to make the call now. Them getting caught couldn't be for nothing. I lurched across the room, balancing speed against stealth.

Once I was sure Lucy's pursuers had left the corridor, I flicked on the torch, shielding the light as much as I could with my body. I found the phone and punched in the number I'd been chanting to myself for two days.

The line crackled, then rang. Once... Twice... Fuck, it was the middle of the night, and Carly was a deep sleeper.

Three rings. Four.

"Come on, Carly. Pick up... pick up..."

"Finn?" Her voice was clogged with sleep, but she knew already it was me.

"It's me. I need help."

"What the fuck, Finn? You drop a pin to somewhere in the middle of nowhere, no explanation, then—"

"Shut up. Just listen!"

Carly fell quiet, listening or pissed off I wasn't sure. I didn't have time to care. "I'm in trouble. Bad. I need you to get me and Dad out of here. This Retreat place is a cult, and they killed a cat, and—"

"If this is a joke, Finn Bryant, it's sick."

"It's not, I swear. Please just come? Please just get us out of here."

There was silence on the end of the line, then Carly's throat clicked. "I'm halfway to you. In a motel. I'll be there in two days, but you're going to have to explain to my mums why I ditched them in the middle of the night."

"I love you. You're the best."

"Remember you owe me once you're back home, okay?"

"Okay." I grinned. I would owe Carly for the rest of my life if she got us out of here. "But you can't drive right up to The Retreat. Leave your car on the road and walk the last few Ks. And you'll have to come at night – after ten o'clock, once the power's out. I'll meet you at the fence in two days. Oh, and there's a box of kittens I'm going to need you to take." The words tumbled out of me, with no care for how ridiculous they sounded. I hoped Carly was taking it in – I hoped she wouldn't be caught before she got here.

"Seriously, what the fuck, Finn?"

I could only shake my head. "I know. That's why I need out."

Thumps sounded in the corridor, then Aria's and Lucy's voices, coming closer.

I shut off the torch. "I gotta go. Love you. Remember – two days' time, after ten." I hung up the phone, not waiting for an answer. Their voices came closer, angry adult ones joining them.

"Ooo," Lucy sing-songed, practically shrieking. "Sending us to Mother's office! We have been bad."

Shit. That was a warning. I spun around in the dark, panic forcing me into movement. No desk, nothing to hide behind... but the cupboard.

I tore across the room, hoping the same magic that had allowed me to find the door earlier would help me find this one. No such luck. My palms hit blank wall. Left or right. Was the cupboard left or right? Right, my head told me, but my head was stupid and had no sense of direction in the dark. I went left, my hand connecting with the cupboard door almost immediately. Thank god for my trust in my inability to trust my instincts.

I fumbled until I found the keyhole and shoved the key into it.

"Is Mother coming?" Aria's voice came through the wall loud and clear, right outside the door. "Should we wait here until she comes?"

"I was just looking for food," Lucy chimed in. "Aria didn't want to come. She was trying to stop me."

Bless them, they really were doing everything they could to give me more time. I skidded into the cupboard, pulling it closed behind me. The sound of the main door creaking open rang out just as I did, and light filtered into the cupboard.

Shit. I'd left the room unlocked. But if any of the adults noticed, they didn't comment on it.

"Mother is coming," a male voice rang out. "Both of you, sit down and don't move until she gets here."

I was safe, hidden, but Aria and Lucy weren't. Was it worth it now, me staying in here? The call was made, Carly was coming. If I came out now, would I save them some grief? Could I convince Mother it was all my influence, no fault on the part of either of my friends? But how would I explain getting into the cupboard, or the torch and key in my possession? So far, no one knew I'd been in here, and Lucy's story about wanting food would surely get them off with a lighter punishment than what we'd really been doing.

I pressed my hand to my mouth, forcing myself to stay silent.

"Aria..." Mother's voice floated through to me in the cupboard, then I heard soft rushed steps crossing the floor.

"I'm sorry." Aria's words were a gasp, fear half swallowing them.

"My baby."

This wasn't what I was expecting. Mother's reactions were always calm, considered, but from the muffled sounds of movement I could hear through the door, I could swear she was hugging Aria, rather than punishing her.

"You!"

I jumped, sure I was caught, but the booming anger now flooding Mother's tone wasn't directed at me.

"We brought you in, took care of you and your family, and you repay me by putting my girl in danger?"

"We weren't in danger," Lucy said. "We were just—"

"Shut up!"

I could practically feel spittle landing on Lucy's face from Mother's shout. What was this? Why was she hugging Aria and screaming at Lucy? Sure, Lucy had taken the blame, but they'd both been creeping around at night.

"She was safe in her bed, and you tempted her from it. You took her away from safety."

"I'm sorry." Lucy's voice shook. I covered my face, scared of what was coming even though I couldn't see it.

"Take her away."

"No, please," Aria said. "She didn't make me, I followed!"

There were sounds of a scuffle, and then I heard a singsonging voice call out as Lucy disappeared down the corridor. "I got in trou-ble. I got in trou-ble."

Man, that girl had guts.

"What about the other one?" the man said.

"Aria..." Mother whispered.

For a moment, she sounded torn. Then the air around us seemed to harden. "You shouldn't have left your bed, Aria. Take her to a repercussion room too."

Chapter Fourteen

I didn't dare move until well after the room outside the cupboard had fallen quiet. I strained my ears to the point where I was sure they'd physically grown at my will. Each time I almost worked up the courage to move, I was sure I heard something – a footfall, a breath, a whimper from one of my friends being hurt. And then I stilled again, waiting, listening, waiting.

Poor Aria. Poor Lucy. The thought of them stuck in that room Aria had described turned my stomach. Would they be together at least? Probably not, given the way Mother came down so much harder on Lucy. What was that about? Just the fact that Lucy wasn't born here? Did she favour her special, Retreat-bred children so much more than the others?

But no, it seemed like more than that. *You repay me by putting my child in danger,* she'd said. *My girl.* There was something so personal about that phrasing.

I shifted, carefully turning myself around in the tight space, and flicked on the torch. I held my breath, waiting to see if my movement or the light had given me away. One breath... two... Still silence from outside the door.

I eased myself up onto my knees. Ironically, now I was actually in the cupboard and had time, plugging my phone in was the last thing I wanted to do. Sure, leaving it here all day would get the battery charged. But there was no way I wanted to risk another midnight break-in to retrieve it. Instead, I returned the papers I'd stolen to the router box then reached for the photo I'd looked at the last time I was in here.

Under my torch beam, Mother smiled down at the baby – the son she'd lost. Or was it? Mother's green dress and the baby's blanket matched the colour Aria most often wore; the colour she'd said Mother would remember.

I pulled the picture from the wall, unfolding it. The shiny photo paper resisted, having been bent for too long. I pressed it flat, smoothing it over my knee. Mother stared down at the baby, and two other figures stared up at me – a little boy, about four or five, and a man with one hand on the boy's shoulder, the other on Mother's back. Both of them had Aria's intensely dark eyes.

Shit.

I flipped the photo over, aiming the torch at the back of it. Cursive writing crawled over the paper, like a line of daddy long legs – "Ackehurst family" and then a date sixteen years ago. Right around the time Aria would have been a baby.

Mother had said our car accidents mirrored each other's. Two halves of a whole, she'd said. She'd meant that more literally than I had thought; mother and daughter killed in one, husband and son dying in the other. It also meant there had been two surviving members of the family in each.

I glanced down at the power outlet. It was so fricken tempting. With the phone charged, I could contact Carly. Maybe even the police. I could open Google and search Ackehurst. But how much would answers cost?

I sighed, leaning my head forward against the shelves. It wasn't worth it.

I pulled out the charger, ready to toss it back in the plastic tub where I'd found it – one less contraband item for me to be caught with.

The cable caught on my pocket and I fumbled, grasping to catch it before it clunked against the floor. I stared at it, something tugging at my memory.

The phone doesn't have to be charged from a wall outlet.

I scrambled to open the plastic tub. It wasn't just filled with phones; I was sure I'd seen laptops in there too. If any of the laptops were still charged, they wouldn't even need to be plugged in...

Something sounded out in the corridor, and I shut off the torch, freezing. Voices filtered through the wall. Not the angry, shouting kind, this time, but soft conversation and laughter.

How long had I been in the cupboard? I bit down hard on my lip, trying to calm myself. I had no sense of time in here. It might be morning already. I should be getting myself out, back to my room, not faffing about on the off chance a laptop I thought I'd seen might have some battery left.

But the phone.

I had to try, if it would help us get out of here.

I lifted the lid of the tub, groping my way through the contents until I found the familiar rectangular shape of a laptop. I pulled it out and opened it up.

Moment of truth. I pressed the power button. Just a little charge. All I needed was just a little charge.

The screen lit up.

I jammed the end of the USB cable into the port. I didn't dare look at what percent the laptop was on. It didn't matter. Something was anything at this point.

"Come on, charge..." I whispered to my phone. I stared at the screen, willing it to work. A logo appeared, along with the charging symbol. "Fuck yeah!"

I froze, instantly regretting my outburst. But there was no sound of running feet, no shouts from the corridor. I was safe, at least for now.

I slumped back against the wall, closing my eyes. Was this worth it? Aria and Lucy getting caught for a call to Carly on the landline and however many percent of battery I could scrounge before the laptop died? I'd better make it be.

The time on the laptop screen was way too close to sunrise for my liking. But then again, maybe that was good. Perhaps I'd be able to join the throngs of people heading to the dining room, staying hidden by blending in. I rubbed a hand across my chin. Hopefully, no one would notice I hadn't showered or shaved.

I pushed the tub back into place, and returned the photo to the wall, fixing it with the pin and nudging the corners back and forth to make sure it was exact. As soon as the laptop died, I'd disconnect the phone and get the hell out of there. Until then, there was nothing to do but wait.

I OPENED THE CUPBOARD door, bracing for darkness on the other side. Unfortunately, darkness was not what I found. Early morning light streamed in around the curtains, like it wanted to personally point me out to Mother and her cronies.

I locked the cupboard behind me, creeping over to the office door. I pressed my back flat against the wall next to it. Footsteps made their way towards me, then away. Then another set coming towards me, then away.

And then silence.

For a moment I froze, but this might be it – the only moment of empty corridor I would get. I hesitated just one second longer, then ripped the door open, hurling myself through it. My phone thumped against my leg with the movement, and I yanked my robe over it automatically.

Door shut, key in the lock, I was almost home free. And then the key stuck.

"Dammit!" I yanked at it, but it held firm. "No!" I couldn't leave it. All Lucy and Aria had sacrificed, all that time I'd spent hidden in that cramped cupboard, it couldn't be undone by this stupid flat piece of metal sticking out of the door like a bright flag screaming "Look at this!"

Someone was coming. Two someones. Footfalls and laughter, coming nearer, and nearer.

"Aha!" The key came loose in my hand. I palmed it, spun on my heel and started walking just as the two someones turned into the corridor. I didn't break my stride, keeping my steps even and casual as I walked towards them. But not towards *them*, of course. I was walking towards the dining hall. I had every reason to be doing that, even though my room was on the other side of the hall, and I had never once walked down this corridor when heading to a meal before.

"Have a safe day," the man said as I reached them. The woman beside him smiled.

"Have a safe day," I echoed, hoping like hell there wasn't another expected response. They passed me, and I let myself exhale when—

"Hey, you're Finn, right? The new kid."

I froze, then slowly turned back, though everything in me wanted to run. "Yeah, that's me." I hoped they didn't notice how high and strained my voice was.

The man frowned. "You don't eat with this group. You eat with Mother."

Was I imagining it, or was this the voice I had heard in the dark last night?

"He's not supposed to be around the younger ones until he's acclimated," he told his companion.

I forced my throat to laugh, my head to shake. "Am I up too early? My stomach was growling, I assumed it must be time to eat. Growing boy, you know." I patted my stomach, cringing internally when my elbow connected with the torch. If they heard it, they didn't give anything away. They both eyed me. They had to have heard about the robes in the bathroom, about my second chance and the special treatment Mother had given me. They had to suspect I was up to something and were perhaps considering the quickest way to get Mother here, to get me to a repercussion room.

"It's not safe for you to be around the kids," the woman said finally. "Go back to your room until it's your turn to eat."

I nodded, then gave an awkward salute. "Yes, ma'am."

I HID MYSELF BEHIND the compost bins to message Carly. My fingers itched to open a search app, and look up what I wanted to know, but every bit of my battery life was precious, and I might need to contact Carly again.

I kept the message simple, praying she'd just accept it without pressing for more details. Who was I kidding? She wouldn't be Carly if she didn't send a million follow up texts.

GOT PHONE BACK. LIMITED BATTERY. LOOK SOMETHING UP FOR ME? ACKE-HURST, CAR CRASH, SIXTEEN YEARS AGO.

A first name for either Mother or Aria's father would help, but I'd take what I could get at this point. I went into my notifications while I waited for Carly to reply. I turned them all off. The kittens made enough noise mewing, doing their best to draw attention to themselves, and I didn't need electronic beeps and buzzes adding to that.

A reply flashed up on my screen: *????*

She must be on the road, unable to type out a proper reply, or to search anything for me. I wrote back, juggling feeding a kitten with the other hand.

THINK THE WOMAN WHO RUNS THIS PLACE WAS INVOLVED. NEED MORE DE-TAILS. PLEASE? TURNING PHONE OFF NOW TO SAVE POWER.

I shut the phone off, as I'd said I would. A wash of fatigue rushed over me. Fatigue, and an unsettling tightness in my chest which I thought might be grief. Not for my mum and Joey – that grief never fully went away. It constantly stretched across my back and arms, pulling tight every time I moved too fast, laughed too loudly, or forgot for even just one moment.

This grief was more like nostalgia, though I wasn't sure I was old enough to feel that. Carly and I used to message every night, though she lived two metres away, and we could see each other through our bedroom windows. I never thought I'd be voluntarily shutting my phone off while waiting for her reply. I'd spent the first two years of puberty convinced I was in love with her, then the years since realising that I just loved her, no *in* about it. She was my best friend, and I missed her. God, I missed her.

I made it back to my room and fed the kittens, finishing just in time for Annabelle's knock on my door. I shoved their box and my phone back in the wardrobe, then stood upright as the door opened.

"Morning, yes, ready to go." I moved quickly through the doorway, cutting off any ideas Annabelle had of coming in.

I stopped short. It wasn't Annabelle, but Angelina standing outside my door.

She smiled at me, that vague, floaty smile. My lips curled in disgust. I'd viewed that smile as peaceful when I first saw it. Now, all I saw was the callous cruelty behind it. Her lack of empathy was what kept her calm. She simply didn't care about anyone else.

"Where's Annabelle?" I asked.

She made a soft "mmm" sound and blinked slowly. "She isn't feeling well. She's gone to the health room."

"Is she okay?"

Angelina made a movement that was almost a shrug. "I'm sure she will stay safe under Mother's care."

Was Mother what passed for a doctor around here? Surely that meant none of us were safe. I thought of Annabelle's tired eyes yesterday, her pinched face. She'd told me the first day I met her that being at The Retreat meant never having to lose anyone again. I wondered if she had instead lost herself.

My own tiredness was catching up with me, not to mention the anxious loops of thoughts about Aria and Lucy.

"Are you well yourself, Finn?" Angelina asked me. "Did you sleep safely?"

It was the same question others asked in the morning, but I could feel Angelina's eyes on me. She knew I'd been involved last night... or not *knew* but suspected. I didn't know how – neither Aria nor Lucy would have given me up, but something made her suspicious of me.

"I slept very well. I dreamed I was a kitten, but someone hurt me, so I turned into a tiger and ate them."

She raised an eyebrow. "How strange. Dreams are such odd things, aren't they?" If she heard the meaning in my words she didn't let on.

MOTHER'S DEMEANOUR didn't betray anything of the night before. She greeted me warmly, squeezing both my hands.

"Are you well, Finn?" she asked. She studied my face like Angelina had, but I didn't think it was with suspicion. A little pucker appeared between her eyebrows, and she rubbed the back of my hand with her thumb.

"Yeah, I'm fine," I said.

She pressed her palm to my forehead. "You're very pale."

I shrugged. "Had strange dreams. Maybe it's that?"

"About tigers, apparently," Angelina chipped in. She'd definitely missed the metaphor.

Mother's frown didn't ease. It confused me to see her so concerned about me. I knew she'd started The Retreat from a good place, but it had become something so twisted and controlling. Was it possible that underneath it all, she still just wanted to protect people?

She pressed my bowl of oatmeal into my hands. "Eat. Some people struggle to adjust to the vegetarian diet. We must make sure you're getting enough calories and protein." She handed me the spoon and watched until I took a bite. No one else was eating yet of course, given we hadn't yet done the weird breathing prayer thing.

But Mother stood, turning to the room rather than the table. Everyone around me fell silent, waiting for her voice.

"A few days ago, I brought you exciting news. I'm afraid today I have an upsetting announcement. One of our younger members, Ada, has been withdrawn from The Retreat."

My head shot up, and a similar ripple went through the room, mutters and whispers passing between tables. Ada... Lucy.

"What does that mean?" I asked Angelina. "Is this – Ada – being sent home?" I pronounced her name carefully, still keeping up the ruse lest I made anything worse for her.

Angelina smiled at me blandly. "Something like that."

Horror rolled through me; the single bite of oatmeal I'd eaten threatening to come back up. *Something like that.* What if they just tossed her out – left her to fend for herself? We were surrounded by kilometres of rough terrain. Lucy was resourceful, but no one is *that* resourceful.

I closed my eyes. *Carly is coming*, I told myself. *Carly will find Lucy and get her help.*

A blonde woman in the centre of the room stood, and the muttered conversations around her fell quiet. She pressed her hands tightly to her lips.

"No," she said, the sound muffled by her fingers. "No. No, no, no, not Lucy!" The words became a scream. "No! You can't. Not my baby!"

I stared at her, feeling like I would pass out. This had to be Lucy's mother. The women on either side of her wrapped their arms around her.

"No!" came her shrieks still, from inside the folds of their embrace. They led her from the room, whispering words that could only be platitudes. I turned back to Mother, but she was watching all this with that benign, peaceful smile on her face, not a shred of the concern she'd shown for me present now.

My head swam. I blinked, and Angelina turned her face towards me. She gasped, reeling back. "He's sick! He's bleeding."

I frowned, her words seeming far away. And they were, as she was still retreating away from my supposed contagiousness. A trickle of sweat ran down my face, and I brushed it away, only then finding the blood she was gasping about. My nose.

Mother gasped too, her hands landing on either side of my face. "No, Aaron, can you hear me?"

Aaron? Who was she talking to? I felt myself droop, the weight of the last few nights crashing over me.

I fell. Down, down, down, into the darkness I'd been running from.

Chapter Fifteen

Webs of cracks spread across the glass in front of me. The smell of petrol made it hard to breathe. I coughed, and tasted blood in my mouth.

I turned, stretching out for Joey's hand. I couldn't reach it. Shards of glass surrounded her, a piece sticking out of her leg. She shrieked, a high repeating scream that stabbed through me.

Mum's breathing was fast. Too fast. Too shallow.

I turned to her. Her face was pale, and her eyes wide. "You have to get out. Go get help, Finn. You have to get out."

Sharp pain stabbed through my chest as I undid my seatbelt. I punched the remaining glass from the side window with my elbow, then pulled myself through the gap, tumbling out onto the ground.

I crawled away from the smell of petrol, and the heat of growing flames. I crawled away from the car, leaving Mum and Joey behind.

WHEN I WOKE, EVERYTHING was quiet and there was a cool hand pressed to my forehead. For a moment I thought it was my mum, and then I remembered and cringed away.

"Shh... sweet boy. It's okay."

My stomach turned at Mother's voice. I shifted, pulling away, but her hand moved with me, stroking my cheek instead. "It's all right, my love. Mother is here."

There was something creepy about the way she said it. The title had always been creepy, but now, it was like she really thought of me as her child. Aaron, she'd called me. Was that his name? The boy in the picture with dark eyes like Aria's? Aria Ackehurst, Aaron Ackehurst... was this where the A names had come from? She was renaming each person who came here, as if adopting them into her brood.

It was more than that with me. The way she looked at me and let me get away with far more than anyone else, the way she'd talked about our car accidents as being two halves of a whole... it was like she really thought I was him. She saw me as Aaron, back from the dead, as if the safety blanket she had wrapped around everyone here had finally performed the miracle she'd been hoping for.

I let her lead me across the grounds to the health rooms, her arm wrapped tightly around me. She put me in one of the beds and pressed her palm to my forehead again, her other hand stroking my face. The touch of her fingers grated like a nail file against my cheek. I couldn't stand it.

Lucy. What had those hands done to Lucy?

I closed my eyes and feigned sleep until it became real.

WHEN I WOKE, MY HEAD felt clearer. I hadn't been sick, I knew that, only burnt out from the nights on covert missions. Now I had rested, I felt fine. Or I did for a moment. Then, the memory of this morning's announcement rang in my ears, along with the sound of Lucy's mother crying out at her expulsion. God. How could I feel rested, when Lucy and Aria had paid the price? Was Lucy already gone? Would her mother follow her, stumbling out into the wild lands after her? And where was Aria? I shuddered at the thought of her trapped in the tight space of a repercussion room.

I sat up, looking around. I wasn't in my own room, but a white space, dimly lit with evening light from the windows. Evening light... shit, that meant the kittens had been alone all day.

"I fed them."

My head snapped around at the voice. Annabelle sat on a chair in the corner of the room, half hidden in shadow.

"Fed who?" I asked.

"The kittens, of course." There was no threat in her words, but there was a hollowness. The dark circles I'd seen under her eyes earlier had deepened, the rims were now red. She rolled a pencil between her fingers, as if it were a cigarette, even bringing it to her lips. She frowned at it, as she tasted wood instead of smoke, and dropped it to the ground, letting it clatter. "You can't keep them in there much longer, Finn. I hope you have a plan."

"You knew?"

She let out a breath in a huff that was almost a laugh. "The smell of cat piss is pretty unmistakeable. I volunteered to walk you in the mornings so no one else would smell it."

I swallowed. I'd been stupid to think I had been getting away with hiding the kittens. This whole thing had been on a knife's edge the entire time I'd been here, and bit by bit I was getting cut. How could everything have gotten so messed up in just a couple of weeks?

"You know, many cultures have superstitions about cats and pregnancy," Annabelle said. "One study even showed a correlation between owning a cat and your baby having schizophrenia. You have to take correlations with a very big grain of salt, of course."

There was more behind Annabelle's words. She had always been soft and gentle, peaceful in a genuine way Mother and Angelina couldn't fake. Now, she felt brittle enough to break.

"You were pregnant, weren't you?" I asked Annabelle.

She nodded, slowly, her whole body rocking with the movement. "And now, I am not. Seven pregnancies, every one of them gone. I thought if I came here, I wouldn't have to lose..." Her voice evaporated into dust.

We won't ever lose anyone again.

I'd seen, in that moment she'd said it, that she truly believed it. Mother had made her all kinds of promises she couldn't keep, and Annabelle had believed them, because she wanted to, because she was desperate, and Mother had preyed on that.

She hadn't been shut away, like Mother said Amelia would be. Annabelle must have hidden the pregnancy. Perhaps her faith in Mother was not so strong after all.

"I shouldn't have come here," she said suddenly. "I wish I was home."

I wanted to tell her about Carly – tell her I had a way to get her out if she'd come with me. But something held me back. The door to this room stood open, the space beyond it wide and echoey. I couldn't be sure who would hear. I couldn't even be sure if I could trust her.

"Do you know what happens if people are withdrawn?" I asked her instead. For a brief moment of hope, I imagined her saying it would all be fine – that someone drove the person to the next town, gave them food and enough money to get to where their family lived, maybe even put them on a train, sending them off with a cheerful wave.

Instead, Annabelle shrugged. "I don't know. They never come back to tell us." She studied my face, her eyes still keen, even if they had hardened with her grief. "I heard about that girl. Did you know her?"

I glanced towards the open door, and Annabelle followed my gaze. She stood slowly, painfully, crossing the room to my bed. I should have gone to her, not forced her to come to me, forced her to drag herself out and care for my kittens.

When she reached me, she lay down next to me, her side pressing against mine. She relaxed a little – not completely, but the flinty edge of tension dropped away.

"I know her," I whispered. "And another girl I'm worried about – Aria."

Annabelle grimaced. "No wonder Ada was withdrawn. Mother is especially protective of Aria. If anyone does anything to threaten her safety..." She tilted her head meaningfully.

"She's Mother's daughter, isn't she? I mean, biologically."

Annabelle stared at me for a long moment, the pieces falling into place for her. "If she is, Aria doesn't know it," she said finally. "Tread carefully, Finn."

I wanted to. I wanted to move gently with Aria, let her make her own decisions about what happened next. But Mother's protective grip would be tightening around us, and I had to get Aria out before we were all strangled by it.

"We meet at night," I told Annabelle. If she was a spy, only pretending to be on my side to gather information for Mother, I had just dumped myself in it. But right now, I had no one else who could help. "I need to get out after lights out – to see if she's okay."

Annabelle nodded. "That can be arranged."

I found her hand and squeezed it. "You would have been an amazing mum. You *will* be one. Families aren't just blood." Families weren't just blood, and neither were mothers – real mothers. I had no doubt Annabelle would find a way to be one.

Her face clouded, and I wondered if that was the wrong thing to have said. She pulled me into a hug. I wrapped my arms around her, holding her gently but tight. "I'm going to get us out of here," I whispered, close to her ear. "All of us. I promise."

I FEIGNED SICKNESS when Mother came to check on me, and she pronounced that I must stay in the health room another night. Annabelle came to my room after lights out. She held a little torch which, she explained, had been given to her so she could find her way to the bathroom in the dark. Apparently, the rest of us were supposed to have iron bladders or eat pureed carrots until we had x-ray vision.

My own stolen torch was back in my room, along with the phone and key. I would have to find a way to get the key and torch into the panel under Mother's seat, but for now, getting to Aria was the priority.

"I've left pillows in my bed. They won't check mine as closely. I'll lie here, so they see you breathing."

It would work if they only looked, but the deception wouldn't hold up to close inspection if Mother decided to come stroke my cheek again.

"Thank you, Annabelle. I couldn't do this without your help."

Annabelle stared at me for a moment, a decision seeming to play out behind her eyes. "Come back in through the far entrance," she said. Her voice had a strain in it, and I tensed. Was she setting me up? Would Mother be waiting for me when I opened that door?

She pulled me into a hug again. "Be safe, Finn. Really, I mean," she added, as she registered her choice of words. She pulled back to look at me. The torch in my hand lit her from below, deepening the shadows in her face. "Jennifer," she told me. "I never thought much of that name, but it's mine, and I should remember it."

I smiled. "Thank you, Jennifer."

IT WAS HARDER TO FIND my way through the dark this time. I wasn't familiar with the position of the health room in relation to the other buildings. I had Annabelle's torch, but out here, it would be like a beacon drawing everyone to me. *For emergencies only*, I told myself.

By the time I'd found my way to the fence, traced along it, and peeled back the metal wire to get underneath, I was scared Aria would have been and gone. If she'd been able to get out at all. I scrambled up on the other side, not wanting to delay any longer.

I followed my way along the river, coming to the pool. I could feel immediately that she wasn't there – hadn't been there in the recent hours.

I'd never known how much the absence of someone could be a sensation in and of itself until I came home from the hospital and Mum and Joey weren't there. The problem wasn't that they were missing, it was that traces of them were still there – Mum's perfume, the weird funky smell that follows little kids no matter how much you make them wash. It made it feel like they were just in the next room, but the next room was cold and dark, the weight of their absence pressing in.

I shouldn't have been able to feel that here, outside, when there was no expectation of light, but it was somehow darker and colder than it should have been. Mother wouldn't let Aria out. She was probably locked in her room, Mother's guards watching her every move. Or she was still in the repercussion rooms. How people didn't lose it in there, I didn't know. I felt my sanity slipping away at just the thought.

I waited anyway, ten minutes, an hour, I wasn't sure. Either way, Aria didn't come.

I trudged back along the bank of the river. It didn't mean anything, I told myself. She hadn't been withdrawn from The Retreat, and Carly was still coming. I would find Aria's room and get her out.

I looked up as a light caught my eye, deep in the bush. I squinted, trying to make it out. "Carly?" I whisper-yelled.

She wasn't supposed to be here for another day, but maybe she'd arrived early. There was no responding whisper. I glanced back towards The Retreat, the thought of Annabelle – Jennifer – lying in my bed, risking her own safety tugged at me. I should get back, let her slip unseen to her own room before anyone found her.

But if that light was Carly...

I hitched my robes up, crossing the river. A sound floated on the breeze, getting louder as I crept towards the light – an out-of-tune singing I was sure I'd heard before. I couldn't make out the words, but my head filled in something in their place. *I got in trou-ble... I got in trou-ble...*

"Lucy?" I called as loud as I dared.

The singing dropped away, silence sharpening the dark, then a soft call came back. "Finn?"

I ran the rest of the way. The light grew in front of me until I could see a building – a building and another fence. The repercussion rooms.

Lucy's face was pressed up against the wire. "Finn!" Her voice rose, excitement filling it. "I knew you'd come. Is your friend here?"

"Shh..." I glanced back towards The Retreat, but Lucy shook her head.

"It's too far for them to hear. They don't want anyone to hear the crying from the repercussion rooms." Her words bounced with excitement. I wanted to vomit at the thought of people crying inside those rooms.

"Carly – my friend – she won't be here until tomorrow, but I can get you out of there now."

Lucy sagged back, hanging from her fingers looped in the wire of the fence. "Don't. They'll know something's up if I'm not here when they come to give me food. Just don't leave without me, okay?"

"Of course not. Carly will get us all out of here."

Lucy nodded. The thought seemed to fortify her. I poked my fingers through the loops of the fence, squeezing her hand. "Are you okay in there?"

She shrugged. "At least they didn't put me in one of the rooms. And they gave me a light." She held up the lantern that had caught my eye through the trees. "They haven't said when they're going to let me come back though."

I frowned. "They didn't tell you? Mother announced you've been withdrawn."

Lucy let out a low whistle. "Withdrawn, huh? Maybe I won't have to wait for Carly to get out of here then. Maybe they're shipping me out tomorrow."

I nodded, but I had a bad feeling it wasn't that simple.

She chewed on her lip. "I'd feel safer leaving with you though. Is my mum okay?"

I thought of her being dragged out from the dining room, calling out for Lucy. "She cried when Mother made the announcement."

"If you get the chance, tell her I'm all right?"

"I will." I'd do everything I could to get the message to her mum. I glanced at the building behind Lucy. "Is Aria in there?"

Lucy shook her head. "Nah, they only locked her up for one night. Mother came and got her herself, hugged her and made her promise never to sneak out again. Went on and on about keeping her children safe."

That sounded about right. "Do you know where Aria's room is?"

"She's in the dummy dormitory normally." Lucy made a face. "Sorry, that's what we call the dorm for the kids who were born here – the ones who don't know anything about the real world. I thought Aria was going to be like them, but she's really smart. She knew something wasn't right about this place, even when they tried to shove the safety down her throat."

The way Lucy spoke, I got the feeling there were others here who felt the same way we did. Others who were itching to get out. I should have told Carly to bring a van.

"You don't think she'll be there now?"

Lucy shook her head. "Mother's so weird about her. She'll put Aria in one of the rooms next to her own. She'll be locked in there, I bet."

That complicated things, but I'd figure it out. I would get them out. If I just kept saying that, it had to become true, right? I would find a way.

"You need to get back," Lucy said.

I nodded, but I didn't move. It felt wrong to leave her here. Dangerous.

"I'll be okay," she said as if reading my thoughts. "You can't get me out of here if you don't go back."

True, but it still didn't feel right. She poked her fingers through the fence, reaching for mine. I grabbed them, squeezing them tight.

"Good luck, Finn. Don't screw up, okay?"

MY DIRECTION SENSE was getting better, and I made it back to the river without any problems. I slowed as I neared the fence. Voices filtered through the night.

"How long has it been like this?" That was Angelina's lilting tone.

"I don't know," a man's voice replied. "I just spotted it when I came back from picking up this week's eggs. That girl must have been sneaking out."

I swore under my breath. The hole in the fence. I hadn't bent the wires back into place; I'd been in such a hurry to see if Aria was waiting for me.

Angelina made an "mmm" sound that in another setting would have been calming. "Mother was right to withdraw her."

"I can fix it, but not until morning. I can do a patch-up job for now."

My heart hammered in my chest. A patch-up job? How good a patch-up job? Hopefully a rough one, given I was on the wrong side of the fence with no other way back.

"Do it. We'll make an excuse about rabbits."

They faffed about at the fence for a long time. I couldn't see what they were doing, but my stomach sank lower with every passing minute. I stayed where I was until the night fell quiet again. Their light disappeared as they went back inside.

I crept back to the fence, taking it a couple of steps at a time, stopping and listening for sounds of alarm being raised. None came. They weren't watching the hole, confident in their belief that they had already caught the culprit. I felt crap at the idea of Lucy being blamed for my sins, but they'd already dealt her their highest punishment. It wasn't like they could do anything worse to her. Besides, I had to remember the end goal. Going unnoticed gave me a better chance of setting her free.

New wires looped through the bottom of the fence, driving down into the earth. I could pull them out, pluck each one from the soil, slip under and then replace them once I was on the other side. It would take time, though, and if I didn't put them back perfectly, any changes would be noticed, surely.

I stepped back, scanning the length of the fence. I hadn't found any other weak points, but I hadn't checked the whole fence since I'd stopped when I found this one. I could continue tracking it, sending up prayers along the way for another opening to materialise in front of me. Again, it would take time... during which the sun would creep higher, ready to peek out behind the hills; time with Annabelle lying in my bed, risking being caught.

I looked up instead, at the full height of the fence.

I had climbed similar ones at school many times. They had never risen this high into the sky, though. Like the dark, I had never been scared of heights, but The Retreat asked me to do things I'd never had to before. I wasn't scared of heights, but everyone is afraid of falling.

It didn't matter; fall or not, I had to try.

I gripped the fence, careful not to yank it, in case the wire creaked, drawing others from their sleep. I'd normally have done this in sneakers, the rubber toes giving additional grip. I couldn't climb in moccasins, so bare feet would have to do. I shoved the soft shoes into the waistband of my boxers, then hooked my toes into one of the wire squares and started to climb.

Halfway up, my forearms burned, and deep indents formed in the balls of my feet where the fence dug into my flesh again and again. *Better grip*, I thought grimly, and kept climbing.

My robes caught as I navigated the top of the fence. I got halfway over, then my feet slipped. For one slow-motion horror moment, I hung from my hands, my fingertips stretching, itching to send me flying. I pedalled desperately, toes searching for a hold, then I crashed against the fence. A shimmer of creaks and groans rang out. Then my right foot finally found purchase through the robe.

I clenched my toes, gripping the fence monkey-like. Someone would have heard; they had to have. I clung, frozen, listening, but all I heard was the pounding of my own heart.

I stared down into the dark, the ground somewhere beneath me. I could survive this drop. My ankles might not, but I could survive it. I just had to have the courage to fall.

I let go. My robes billowed around me like a useless parachute, and then the ground was underneath me. Shock waves rippled up my limbs. I bit down on my lip, silencing the urge to cry out. I'd landed in a crouch, hands forward, and it was my right wrist not my ankles that screamed in pain. *Easier to hide*, I told myself. It was little comfort when I tried to move my fingers and couldn't.

I couldn't stay here, either.

I forced myself up, made myself limp in the direction of the health room. A door opened somewhere behind me. I flattened myself into the shadows, back to creeping along walls like a rat.

A torch beam shone over the patch of fence where I had just been. "A bird must have hit it," an unfamiliar woman's voice said.

"Stupid creatures," came the reply. "Don't bother putting it in the report or she'll make us cull them again."

I let out a breath and kept creeping.

Chapter Sixteen

I made my way around the side of the health room, heeding Annabelle's warning to come in the back way. Again, the choking fear of a setup had me freezing on the doorstep. Annabelle was on my side, I reminded myself. Mother had had hours to catch me, and I was still free.

I eased the door open, clutching my damaged arm to my chest under my robes. The irony of trying to hide an injury in the place meant to treat it wasn't lost on me. Perhaps I could steal a bandage or some painkillers. If they had painkillers here, that was. It wouldn't surprise me if it was all clove oil and willow bark tea.

Glow-in-the-dark strips lined the corridor in this part of the building, and I let out a breath. Perhaps this was why Annabelle had suggested I come in this way. I followed the meagre light they gave off, guessing at the way back to my room.

Voices floated out of an open doorway ahead, and I froze. A flickering light came from inside – the unmistakeable glow of a TV. Was there power in this part of the building? I hesitated, then crept towards the room.

It wasn't a TV, but a laptop playing videos. A man sat in a lazy boy chair in front of it. An IV pole stood beside him, the bag dripping into a line in his arm. So, I was wrong about the willow bark tea – The Retreat didn't completely shun modern medicine. I suppose they couldn't, with all Mother's chants of safety.

I leaned forward to get a better look at what he was watching, and my wrist brushed against the doorframe, sending a shock of pain through me. I gasped, then clapped my good hand over my mouth. My eyes flew to the man, but he hadn't moved, his gaze remaining glued to the screen. Or was it? His head lolled at an odd angle, broad shoulders tilting sideways, as if whatever was in that IV bag had knocked him out quickly, with no time to settle comfortably before sleep took hold.

There was something familiar about the lines of his limbs, the curve of his neck and the side of his ear. Fear built inside me. A bubble of it grew out and up. I knew that if it reached my mouth I would scream.

"Dad?" I said.

He didn't answer, didn't look up. His head still lolled against his shoulder.

"Dad?" I circled the lazy boy, stepping between him and the screen.

His eyes were open, staring. There was a smile on his face, between clean-shaven cheeks. The face was both familiar and unfamiliar, made up of old and new pieces.

I glanced at the laptop. Mum's face smiled back at me, then mine, then Joey's. Old videos and photos from Dad's phone danced across the screen.

I closed my eyes, not ready to look at those yet. Maybe I would never be able to see their faces happy again – not without also seeing their end replay in my mind.

I sank down onto the floor beside Dad's chair. "Dad? Hey, Dad, it's me. Can you hear me?" I shook his shoulder.

He turned towards me, his eyes taking a long time to focus. "Joey?"

"No, it's me. Finn."

Joey and I looked alike, but not so much that anyone would muddle us up. The age gap between us was too great, not to mention the gender difference.

Dad's smile grew. "Finn..." he said.

I leaned my forehead against his arm. He didn't react, the limb remaining limp under my touch. His gaze was already drifting back to the screen, to the pretend little world where everything was still perfect.

I LEFT HIM THERE. OF course I did. I was always leaving people I cared about. But what else could I do? He was basically catatonic, with or without the IV, I suspected. No wonder I hadn't seen him since we arrived. On some level, I had lost him the day Mum and Joey died, but this was another step – another thing torn from me.

I dragged my uninjured hand down my face as I limped along the corridor. Maybe this was a good thing. At least this way, I wouldn't have to fight him to make him leave with me and Carly. I had a feeling if I picked up that screen and walked away with it, I could lead him anywhere I wanted.

The glow-in-the-dark strips stopped before I got to my room, but my feet found the way, some internalised compass now switched on. It wasn't left and right that guided me now, but North and East, some primal instinct activated by desperation and darkness.

Annabelle didn't stir as I opened the door. She was curled on her side under the blankets, her figure believable as mine. The only movement was the slow rise and fall of her breaths. I wondered if she'd slipped into sleep.

"It's me," I whispered, moving closer to the bed.

She sat up, rousing instantly. "Finn, thank god." She pulled me into a hug, and I stifled a yelp, the pain in my arm screaming. She drew back. "What's wrong? Did they catch you?"

I shook my head. "No one saw me. But I had to climb over the fence. I think my wrist is broken." There were gaps in that explanation, but I didn't have the energy to fill them. Annabelle's hands were on me instantly, easing my arm from its cradled position against my body.

"Jesus, Finn," she whispered. She guided me to the bed, pushing me to lie down. "I can stabilise it, but we need to get you to a hospital."

"Did you know my dad was down there?"

Annabelle didn't look up, her focus on my injury. "I did. He's been there since you arrived."

"Why didn't you tell me?" My voice rose up, and Annabelle pressed a finger to my lips, shushing me. I shrugged away from her. We were back to the beginning – her forcing me into silence.

"I didn't think it would be helpful, earlier, when I thought you'd both stay. Tonight, I knew you'd forget about going out to meet Aria if you found out he was here, and I couldn't let you do that. It was better you found him when you came in through the back door."

"How long...?" I cut that thought short. The answer meant nothing when time blurred the way it had since I'd been here. "What's wrong with him?" I asked instead.

Annabelle sighed. "He's grieving."

"We've been grieving for a year. It's more than that."

Annabelle studied my face in the low light. "The thing is, I don't think you *have* been grieving. Either of you."

Annabelle had told me to use the silence – to let it heal me. Instead, I'd spent the last week in a rush of frenetic energy, trying desperately to escape. Escape The Retreat... Escape myself... Was this what she had meant? Was Dad's vacant stare what she saw as healing?

"Your father broke down when there were no more distractions to keep him from feeling the full force of his grief. My team weren't equipped to deal with the intensity of his emotions. I had to sedate him."

"*You* had to sedate him?"

"I was a doctor before I came here – a psychiatrist." Annabelle gave a joyless laugh. "I know, not the type of person you would expect to run away from their life like this."

I'd thought the same about Dad – physicists weren't normally the type of people to get sucked in by cults. Not that I knew any other physicists... or had experience with cults other than this one.

"I just saw so much pain... so many people disconnected from each other by the modern world. I guess I thought..." She trailed off, shaking her head. "I don't know what I thought."

I let the silence hang for a moment – let Annabelle process her own grief and questionable life choices. I could see how it could happen. The Retreat promised a lot of things that would appeal to a person. Promised, but didn't deliver.

"Will you help me with him?" I asked her. "Will you help me get Dad out of here when my friend comes?"

She gave a half nod, setting her mouth into a grim line. "When?"

"Tomorrow. I'll get us all out then."

Annabelle didn't say anything, just set to work on my wrist. *Tomorrow.* I could make it work, couldn't I? They were all in different places – Dad, Aria, Lucy and the kittens – but somehow, I would draw them together, bundle us into Carly's car, and escape all of this.

Chapter Seventeen

My wrist throbbed the next morning. Annabelle had done her best, fashioning a splint out of a spoon and strips of fabric torn from the end of the bedsheet. Someone would find the frayed edge eventually, but hopefully we would be long gone by the time they did.

Mother came to visit me after breakfast. "How are you feeling, Finn?" she asked. "Did you sleep safely?"

"Yes, I slept safely, thank you." It pained me to phrase it like that, to parrot back the word "safely" when I knew this place was nothing of the sort. Mother's smiled stretched, though, and I knew it had been the right choice.

"I'm glad," she said. "You know, I think you may be nearing the end of your acclimation period."

Even though I knew it would never come to pass, that I would be gone well before she decided I was acclimated, the thought still sent my insides into a double-time churn. I couldn't be acclimated here, ever.

"Can I go back to my room?" I asked. "I feel much better now."

Mother pressed her hand to my forehead, and I forced myself to stay still, to not cringe away. "Are you sure you wouldn't like to stay here another day, Aaron? To make sure you are truly well?"

I froze at the name, bile rising in my throat. "I'm sure, Mother," I choked out. "It's hard to sleep here. I kept thinking I could hear a TV."

She didn't react to my reference to my father, stroking my forehead instead. "You'll sleep better in your own bed, darling."

I FED THE KITTENS, who were thankfully all fine thanks to Annabelle's intervention, then snuck out to the compost bins again to check my phone. A string of messages from Carly lined my screen.

- NEARLY THERE. WILL ARRIVE TONIGHT AT 10.

- LIGHT'S OUT AT 10, RIGHT? OR WAS IT 10.30?

- ????

- FINN?

- MESSAGE WHEN YOU GET THIS.

- SERIOUSLY, FINN. WTF WITH THIS ACK-EHURST FAMILY? NEED TO GET YOU OUT OF THERE.

That last message freaked me out. What had she found? I only had ten percent battery left, so I sent a quick reply confirming lights out was at 10pm, then shut the phone off and returned to my room.

I lay down in the bed. *Just for a minute.* I would lie here just for a minute, then I had to find Aria. I had to figure out that last piece of the puzzle to get us all free.

I WOKE WITH A START. The angle of the light at the window told me it was already afternoon. The kittens mewed, asking for more milk, and I dragged myself up. At least there was still electricity. If I'd slept past lights out and missed Carly, I never would have forgiven myself.

Once the kittens had had their fill, I slipped my injured wrist inside my robe then stepped out into the yard. Lucy had told me Aria would be in a room by Mother's, but I'd forgotten to ask one crucial piece of information – where *was* Mother's room?

I took a walk anyway, hoping I would find it. I'd never even been inside the regular dormitories, Mother's desire to keep me from the children forcing me away. I knew they were in the large buildings at the centre of The Retreat, though, and I headed in that direction.

My steps slowed as I passed the gap in the fence. Sturdy metal clips had replaced the thin wires; no more patch-up job. There was no way I'd get through now.

I walked a few more paces before that really sank in.
Fuck.

I couldn't climb over the fence with an injured hand. Even without that, I couldn't do it carrying a box of kittens.

Annabelle wasn't strong enough after her miscarriage, and I'm guessing Aria had no idea how to scale a fence.

We were so close, *Carly* was so close, and now a stupid fence was going to keep us from running. The unfairness of it all ground into me, and I sucked in air through my teeth to stop myself screaming.

I had to get to Aria. There had to be another way through the fence. The list of things that were just out of my reach started to pile up.

Then again, one of those problems might be the answer to the other. If there was another way out, even a rumour of one, surely Aria would know about it.

A woman pacing the yard caught my eye. The ends of blonde hair poked out from below her hood, but it was more than that. There was something about her slow steps, the angle of her head tilted towards the ground, that ached of sadness. I'd got better at recognising people, despite the shapeless robes, and that thought terrified me. I didn't want to get used to anything here.

I sighed. I needed to get to Aria, but I had promised Lucy.

I ambled my way over to the woman, keeping my stride unhurried. I fell into pace beside her. She straightened a little, matching her steps to mine. It was something I'd seen people here do – quietly walk together in simple moments of connection. If it wasn't for everything that surrounded those moments, I would have thought it was a beautiful thing.

"Are you Ada's mother?" I asked. I didn't dare use her real name, in case I was wrong.

The woman stiffened but kept walking. "We do not speak of those who have been withdrawn." Her voice was tight with unspilt tears. That seemed like confirmation enough.

"I saw her," I whispered. "Out in the repercussion rooms."

The woman froze. Her head was angled away from me. I wanted to dip mine to catch a glimpse of her face, but I couldn't risk drawing attention to us.

"She told me to tell you she's okay. She said to tell you *Lucy* is okay."

The woman breathed in sharply. Her eyes flicked up, finally meeting mine. So many emotions raced across her features, none of them settling before the next one took over.

I almost told her about our plan to leave, but caution set in at the last second. I would find her, though, when everything was ready. I'd give her the option to get out of here.

"I have to go," I told her. "I just wanted to tell you I'm sorry about what happened to her. To both of you."

Lucy's mother didn't say anything, just kept staring. Her eyes flickered with confusion, sadness and fear. Perhaps they all came down to one emotion – grief. It didn't always have to follow a death to overwhelm you.

I backed away, leaving her standing in the middle of the grounds.

I made my way to the grassy area in front of the dormitory blocks. Kids played on the field, their games closely resembling those I'd played at primary school but... different somehow. The kids themselves looked like any other group of young people. Apart from the robes, they could have been from my old school, hanging out during the lunch break.

The longer I watched, the more I noticed the way they moved was different too – more gangly and uninhibited. Was this one of the benefits of The Retreat I'd been promised? The children growing up without the self-conscious pressures of the world?

It didn't outweigh the downsides.

I was pretty sure these were the precious kids – the ones who had always lived here. The fact that I'd never seen a single one of them out in the main yard, and that almost all of them wore pale green robes, seemed like pretty big clues. Funnily enough, the robe Mother had given me this morning was green too. I didn't like to think what that meant from her point of view, but from mine, she'd just given me the perfect cover to get in here.

I slipped into the grassy area, keeping my head low.

As usual, the robes made it hard to pick out features. Judging by height alone, the kids sitting and standing around the entrance to one of the buildings were about my age. Perhaps that meant this was their dorm – Aria's dorm, if she ever made it back here.

I didn't approach the group. If there had been just one kid, I could have got away with hiding my face. But a whole group of them, and they'd pick me as a stranger straight away.

I waited until a kid broke away from the others, heading down the path and into the bathroom block. I trailed after him, not approaching until after he'd come out again. Stopping him from relieving a full bladder wouldn't exactly have endeared me to him.

"Hey," I said.

"Hey…" His voice held a hesitancy. His head shifted slightly as he tried to catch sight of my face. I kept it lowered, letting the hood droop down to cover my features. He didn't seem suspicious, perhaps used to playing a guessing game to recognise his contemporaries.

"You seen Aria?" I asked, keeping my tone light.

He didn't respond for a moment, then he leaned back against the wall behind us. I joined him, resting back as if casually contemplating the view.

"She's still locked in beside Mother. Another day, I've heard, but they reckon she'll be out tomorrow."

So, the rooms beside Mother's were another regular consequence – something they were all used to seeing happen. Of course, Mother wouldn't see it as a punishment. She'd think it was a protection. A safeguard.

Another day. That meant I wouldn't be able to get to her before Carly arrived. Could I ask Carly to wait longer? To camp out in her car and come back for us? It was too much, especially after everything she'd already done.

But I already knew I would ask it of her anyway. I'd have to.

The boy beside me leaned closer, and I shifted my hood automatically.

"You're him, aren't you? The new kid."

"I… I don't…" No excuse came to me. How stupid had I been to think I could fool a bunch of people who had lived together their entire lives? I stood, ready to run, but the boy reached out, grabbing my forearm.

"Word is you're going to get Aria out?"

I hesitated. No accusation lined his voice, only curiosity. I leaned back against the wall, but only lightly, ready to spring up again if my first instinct to run proved correct. "And if I am?"

The boy let out a low whistle. "Then I want to come too."

"Really?"

He nodded eagerly. "Someone snuck in a book. I didn't know all the words, but it talked about a metal building that can fly. I forget the name."

"Aeroplane?" I supplied, and he nodded so vigorously his robe slipped back, revealing bright, excited eyes and curly red hair underneath.

"That's it! Have you ever seen one?"

I grinned. "Kid, I've flown in one."

"No way! I want to learn to fly one. A pi-ot, I think it was called."

I shook my head. Even kept away from the world, it had found them. I had a pretty good idea of what Mother would think of him becoming a pilot. I frowned as something occurred to me. "Wait, you've never seen a plane? You don't see them flying overhead?" I glanced up at the sky as if one would appear. When was the last time I'd seen something soaring past? Or even heard the engines?

He shrugged. "No. We never see anything fun out here."

I knew we were in the middle of nowhere, but I hadn't fully realised until that moment quite how remote we were. If Carly didn't find us, no one ever would.

"There are others too – who want to leave, I mean," the boy said. "How many of us can you take?"

I frowned. Carly's car was tiny – it would barely hold me, Dad, Annabelle, Lucy and Aria. But I couldn't leave people trapped here. "I'll do my best to find a way out for anyone who wants one." It might not be in the first trip, but I could call the police once I was out – or come back myself. Whatever I had to, I would do it, but I had to make sure Lucy and Aria were safe first. They were the ones in the most danger right now.

"Thank you," the boy said. "They'll all be so excited."

"Don't tell anyone," I said quickly. "You can't. Not yet. You'll put me and my friend at risk. We can't get you out if you tell everyone."

He nodded solemnly. "Secrets. I'm good at those."

And maybe he was, if he'd managed to keep a book about aeroplanes quiet.

"Is there any way I can talk to Aria?" I asked him. "Any way I can get her out?"

He frowned. "Talk to, maybe. Get her out, no." He straightened up. "Let me check things out first. Stay here – I'll be back."

I WAITED, WATCHING the kids play while the boy ran off into one of the dorms. I kept my hood low, and no one paid me any attention. In the green robe, I was just another one of them.

My hand was throbbing, and a similar pulse pounded in my ears. If I listened too hard, I could almost hear words in it.

I hadn't asked the boy's name, but I reckoned I'd probably be able to guess it, given enough chances – Arthur... Able... Abraham... How many A names could there be? What a strange little world Mother had created here.

Suddenly, the boy reappeared beside me. I blinked. I hadn't seen him approach, but maybe my eyes had glazed over, mistaking one robed figure for another.

"Come on. I can get you into the room next to Aria's, and you can talk to her through the wall."

I grinned. "You're a genius."

He shook his head, solemnly. "No, I'm a pi-ot."

I didn't have the heart to correct him.

"What's your name?" I asked, as he led me into one of the dorms.

He hesitated. "Aria always says we shouldn't use names when we're doing something we shouldn't. That way Mother can't make us tell on anyone else if we're caught."

That made sense. The robes hid faces, so lack of names could guarantee anonymity. I'd always known Aria was smart, but the level of thought she put into everything still surprised me sometimes.

"But I suppose you might need it to get me out. It's Anthony. My friends call me Tony, though. We're sick of the As."

I had to laugh. Small rebellions. They built up to a lot when you had nothing else.

"In here," Tony said, opening the door to an empty bedroom. "Knock on that wall, and Aria will hear you. You think you can find your own way out?"

"Yeah, I'll be okay." If I could navigate in the pitch black of night, this would be a piece of cake. Tony nodded and left me to it. I stared at the wall. A neatly made bed leaned up against it, as if inviting me to sit while Aria and I spoke.

She was just on the other side of that wall, in the room right next to me. It took everything in me to stop myself from storming back out into the corridor and ripping her door open with my bare hands. If I did that, we'd have about two seconds before she was locked back up, and I was out in the forest with Lucy, either in a repercussion room or withdrawn.

Instead, I crossed the room, rapping on the wall lightly with my knuckles – my uninjured hand of course. "Aria?" I called.

Her feet thumped against the floor as she raced to meet me on the other side of the wall. "Finn? Tony said you were coming, but I wasn't sure if he was teasing me."

"It's me." There was so much I wanted to say, though I would have preferred to do it with her next to me, her body pressed against mine as we huddled for warmth in the forest. Or not in the forest. One day, maybe we would sit together on a couch, both of us freed from this place. Maybe one day, I would even be able to kiss her again.

Right now, there were other things that had to be said – questions I had to ask. "Is there another way out? They found the gap under the fence."

Even through the wall, I heard her gasp. "Do they know it was us?"

"No. They think it was Lucy – Ada. But Carly's coming tonight. Is there another way to get out to her?"

Aria was quiet for a long time. "No," she said finally. "I don't know of one."

My breath came out in a rush. I leaned forward, pressing my forehead against the wall. I could almost imagine her doing the same on the other side, pressing against the same spot.

"Finn... you'll have to go without me."

I shot up. "What? No. We'll wait."

"Mother won't let me out of here until tomorrow. If your friend is coming tonight, then—"

"Then we'll wait. I'll find a way to give her the kittens tonight, and she'll come back for us tomorrow." I wasn't leaving another person behind. Joey's face floated into my head, and I pushed it away. I couldn't think about her right now.

Aria was quiet for such a long time, I thought she wasn't going to say anything else. Finally, I heard the tap of her leaning against the wall. "Get her to take Ada tonight too. Come back for me tomorrow, but get Ada out tonight, okay?"

I nodded at the wall. "Okay."

Chapter Eighteen

None of it had come together. I was here, inside the fence with no way to get free, while Carly would be outside. Aria was locked in the dorm, Lucy stuck by herself in the repercussion rooms, and Dad and Annabelle in the health room. All I could do was go meet Carly, hand her the kittens – somehow – and hope that she could find Lucy in the dark.

I MESSAGED HER, JUST after 10pm: *I'M BY THE GATE*.

A tick appeared, and then the screen went black, battery dead again. No matter. At this point, Carly was either here or she wasn't. There wasn't a whole lot else I could do about it either way.

Carly didn't appear... and didn't appear and didn't appear. I leaned my forehead against the wire, hope fading.

"Finn?" Her soft voice was unmistakeable.

"Carly Throw," I whispered back.

"Seriously, what the fuck, Finn? This place is weird as—"

"I know."

"So let's get out of here."

I shook my head. "I can't. I can't get the others out until tomorrow." *If then...*

"Others? How many people are you bringing with you?"

"As many as I can." I nearly said, "As many as want to come," but that wasn't true. I had no idea how many of those there would be, and we wouldn't be able to take everyone.

"Finn… this is crazy. My mums know I'm here, and they're on their way. I couldn't fob them off any longer. They're probably going to turn up with a bunch of cops, so just come with me now, okay?"

A bunch of cops might not be such a bad idea. I held up my splinted wrist. "Even if I wanted to, I can't climb the fence, but I've got the kittens. I think I can get them under and—"

"What. The actual. Fuck. Finn."

I closed my eyes. "I know." It was nuts, all of it. I'd had no real plan other than getting Carly here. I'd just assumed it would all come together. I leaned my head against the fence again, and after a moment, I felt Carly do the same on the other side.

"I searched that name," she said quietly. "You said it had something to do with the woman who runs this place?"

"Ackehurst?" Honestly, I'd pretty much forgotten I'd asked her to do that. "You find anything?"

She nodded. "Yeah. Weird stuff."

"How so?"

"The little boy – Aaron – died in a car accident. The mother went a bit mad, wouldn't let anyone in the house, spent all day on online forums, started spouting all this stuff about safety, doing weird things she said were to 'protect' her baby."

"That sounds about right."

"Then she and the daughter disappeared, leaving the husband behind. You really think it's the woman who runs this place?"

"Wait, what?"

"Which part?"

"Left the husband behind – he didn't die in the car accident?"

Mother had never actually said that, but I'd assumed so, when she said our accidents mirrored each other's.

"No, very much still alive. I called him; he said he'd never heard of this place, but he's been searching for his daughter for years."

"You talked to Aria's dad? Could you get him here?"

"Aria? You mean the daughter's here? I kind of figured the mother would have killed her or something."

"She's here. Alive. She's our age now."

Aria had a father. Maybe everything wasn't lost.

"You have to call him again," I said. "You have to get him to come and get her out."

Carly was quiet for a moment. "Okay, I'll try. But please, Finn, can you just come with me now?"

I shook my head. "I really can't..." I hesitated. Carly wasn't going to like this bit. "And there's something else I need you to do."

"Jesus, Finn. What do you want now? One of my kidneys?"

"Only the left one," I said automatically, and I felt rather than saw her grin.

She let out a breath. "What is it? What do you need me to do?"

"There's a girl – out in the forest. She's in another building. There's a fence like this one around it. I need you to get her out."

"By myself?!"

"I know. I shouldn't ask you to do that, but I'm stuck in here."

Carly let out a sound that was almost a laugh. "I reckon I can help with that." She slid off her backpack, and opened it, pulling out a pair of bolt cutters. "I figured we might need these when you said you were trapped. Spent forty bucks on them – nearly cleared out my bank account on stuff for this trip." She grinned again. "You owe me, Finn Bryant. Big time."

CARLY WAS ALL FOR CUTTING the lock on the gate, but I persuaded her we needed to go with something more subtle.

"I've got to go back in there. I can't make it obvious that I left."

"All right," she said with a sigh. She knelt down, snipping the wires at the base of the fence a few metres from the patched-up hole. This time, I would remember to bend the wires back into place, covering my tracks. I pushed the box of kittens through the gap, then crawled under myself.

"You keep saying you can't leave, but... Oohh." Carly cut herself off as she peered down into the box. "When you said kittens, I thought you meant... well, I don't know what I thought you meant, but not literal cats."

"Yup, literal, fully alive, not dead cats."

Carly's nose wrinkled. "We'd be having a different conversation if you'd just handed me a box of dead kittens."

I shook my head. "Schrödinger's cat...? It's a long story," I added when she looked blank.

The cats were alive and would stay that way as long as Carly could get them out of here. "Come on. We have to go help my friend."

Carly stumbled through the dark, and I put my arm around her, guiding her just like Aria had me. Carly carried the box of kittens, partly because of my busted hand and partly because once I handed her a pile of sweet, fluffy faces, I knew there was no way she was giving them back.

"So this Aria..." Carly asked as we walked.

"We have to cross the river here," I said, ignoring the unspoken question. I stepped out across the river myself, reaching back to help Carly over. She skipped across like we were playing pooh sticks in the park.

"Should I be jealous?" she asked.

I blinked at her. "Of Aria? She's locked in a room next to her cult-leader mother right now, so..."

"You know what I mean. Is she cute? Girlfriend or friend?"

"Can we talk about this after we escape?"

Carly huffed out a breath. "Well, that would be tonight, if you weren't insisting on going back for her, so... I guess that makes it girlfriend."

Did it? Honestly, I didn't know. Given the whole "not knowing she shouldn't get naked in front of people" thing, I suspected I'd have to explain what a boyfriend was before Aria could decide if she wanted me to be one. That was, if she could even cope with something like that once her whole world was turned upside down by us leaving here. All that was far too complicated to explain right now though, so instead, I nudged Carly with my shoulder. "Friend or girlfriend, you don't need to be jealous. You'll always be *best* friend, Carly Throw."

She nudged my shoulder back, then made a noise in her throat. "Barf. Don't go getting all squishy on me, Finn Bryant."

The lights from the repercussion room came into view. "Shh, we're nearly there."

Carly grumbled for a second about being shushed, then fell quiet. Around us, the rustling sounds of night pressed in, undeterred by our presence. Something about that bothered me. A warning fired in the back of my mind, but I couldn't quite grasp hold of it. I tried to shake it off. We had to get Lucy out.

We crept forward, the building becoming clear in front of us.

"What's that sound?" Carly whispered.

I half turned. Churning nausea built in my stomach once again. The sound was a regular thunk, like a shovel hitting soil, but that wasn't the only thing which had me wanting to throw up. That warning firing in my head? It was the *lack* of a particular sound. Lucy wasn't singing.

"Shit." I surged forward.

"Finn, wait!" Carly hissed behind me. I didn't stop. I raced towards the repercussion rooms. I desperately wanted to see Lucy standing at the fence, her fingers looped through the wire, waiting for me. Instead, a crumpled shape lay at the base of the fence. It took me a moment to spot Lucy's hand, pale and still beside her.

"No. No, no, no, no, no!" I scrambled to pull back the wire at the base of the fence, squeezing my arm underneath. "Lucy, come on, wake up. You have to wake up!"

She didn't move.

"Lucy!" I grabbed her wrist. Everything froze for a moment. Her skin was icy cold, no hint of a pulse under my grip.

I jerked back, scrambling away from the fence. A howling shout built in my stomach, ready to roll up and out through my lips. Carly crashed into my shoulder. Seconds later her hand clamped down over my mouth. I screamed into her hand, my eyes going wide as she dragged me back.

"Shut up, Finn. Just shut up," she hissed.

I couldn't. Lucy was dead. They'd killed her. *Withdrawn* her. She was dead. Stuck in the box forever.

"Finn, please!" Carly's fingers bit into my cheek.

I sucked in a breath. It came in ragged, and I realised I was crying.

"Finn, we have to get out of here. That sound... I think they're digging a grave."

The thunk continued, the rhythmic beat of it unchanged. I ripped Carly's hand away from my face, and threw up in the bushes. I'd left Lucy in the repercussion rooms. I'd left her there, just like I'd left Mum and Joey, and now they were going to bury her out here.

"Finn..."

"I left her," I said.

Carly pressed her hands to the sides of my face, but I couldn't see her. All I could see was that web of cracks spread out across the windshield.

Go get help, Mum had said. *You have to get out, Finn. Go get help.*

I shouldn't have left them. I should have dragged Joey out with me and run with her to the nearest hospital. I should have pulled the car door from the frame and made a gap big enough to pull Mum through. I should have climbed over that fence and got Lucy out of there. I should have done anything other than left them.

"It's not your fault." Carly wrapped herself around me. She was shivering badly, her whole body tremoring. "You tried to help her."

"I left her. I left her, just like I left Mum and Joey."

Carly pulled back, pressing my face between her hands again. "You know that's not true, Finn."

"It is. I crawled out of that car to save my own skin and just left them there."

Carly shook her head, fiercely. "No. There was nothing you could have done."

There was blood on Joey's hand. Her nails had started to turn blue. I heard the high-pitched shriek, and the too fast, too shallow breathing.

"I left them," I said again. "I left them, and the car caught fire."

Mum's face was so pale, and her eyes were wide. Wide... and unblinking.

"Finn..." Carly said slowly. "Your mum and Joey both died on impact, you know that."

Go get help... You have to get out, Finn. Go get help.

I stared at Carly. That's what the coroner's report had said – that Mum and Joey both died on impact.

But if that was true, why did I remember Joey shrieking? If they were both dead before I climbed out of the car, why did I remember Mum telling me to go?

WEBS OF CRACKS SPREAD across the glass in front of me. The seatbelt cut into my neck, pinning me against the headrest. The smell of petrol made it hard to breathe. I coughed, and tasted blood in my mouth.

I turned, stretching out for Joey's hand. I couldn't reach it. A single trickle of blood ran down her fingers, over the edge of her booster seat, onto the upholstery.

Shards of glass surrounded her, a piece sticking out of her leg. Her head lolled to the side, bent at an unnatural angle.

I shrieked, a high repeating scream that stabbed through me. My breathing was fast. Too fast. Too shallow.

I turned to Mum. Her cheek pressed against the steering wheel, her eyes open and wide and staring. Her side of the car was completely caved in, crushing her body. The truck that hit us wedged up against her. Twisted pieces of metal stuck out and into her like claws.

I touched Joey's wrist, moving aside the shattered glass to press my fingers to her vein. She had no pulse.

I screamed again, and again. It was then that I smelt the smoke, mixing with the petrol fumes.

You have to get out, I told myself. *You have to get help.*

I told myself I was going to get help, because it was the only way I could make myself move. I told myself someone would be able to save Joey and Mum.

Sharp pain stabbed through my chest as I undid my seatbelt. I punched the remaining glass from the side window with my elbow, then pulled myself through the gap, tumbling out onto the ground.

I crawled away from the smell of petrol, and the heat of growing flames. I crawled away from the car, leaving Mum and Joey's dead bodies behind.

CARLY WRAPPED HER ARMS around me once more. "Please come with me, Finn. We'll take the kittens and go, now."

I shook my head. "I can't leave them," I whispered.

I was the one shrieking.

I had been breathing too fast and too shallow.

"You have to," Carly whispered.

I heard Mum's voice because I had known I had to get out of the car. Because I would have died there too if I hadn't.

I pulled back from Carly's hug. She stared at me, her eyes desperate, but I think she understood.

"Tomorrow," I said. "Tomorrow, I will go with you."

She hesitated, then nodded, once, her head barely moving with the gesture.

"Bring the police," I told her. "And Aria's dad, if you can." We would need everyone we could get on our side if this was going to work. "We're not leaving anyone behind."

Chapter Nineteen

Carly walked back to the fence with me. "I'm going to ask one last time—"

"I'm not coming with you," I said. "But I will see you very soon," I added, before she could protest.

She nodded. "Police, Aria's Dad, probably both my mums – the cavalry will get you out of there." She pulled me into a one-armed hug, the kitten-box balanced on her hip.

"Ow." I pulled my injured hand out of the way. "Careful, Carl."

"You'll live. And don't call me Carl." Her face went serious, probably remembering Lucy hadn't lived. Another wave of grief swept through me. I had to get the others out.

Carly waited while I rolled under the fence, then pressed her hand to the wire mesh. "Tomorrow," she said.

"Tomorrow. Now get those kittens out of here. The sun will be up soon."

Carly stepped away from the fence, walking backwards a few paces before turning around. I watched until she disappeared into the trees, then crouched down, bending the wires back into place. It wasn't perfect, but it would pass a quick inspection. At least, I hoped it would.

My stomach still churned a little, and I wondered if I should try to throw up one more time before I collapsed in my bed. It felt like too much effort. I dragged myself back to my room, and lay face down on the mattress. The silence from the wardrobe gave me mixed feelings. I was glad the kittens were safe – actually safe – but they had been the anchor keeping me sane. I missed their faces already. I missed the routine of feeding them. More than that, I missed Lucy.

I shook my head. I couldn't let myself think about her, or I would fall apart. We had to get out first.

It's okay to sleep, now, I told myself. *You've done everything you can.*

I WOKE AT THE SOUND of a fist hammering against my door. It flew open before I could even sit up.

"Get up!" Annabelle yanked my arm, pulling me from the bed.

"Ow! I'm up, I'm up. What's going on?"

Annabelle bent forward. She clutched a hand against her stomach, her whole body a giant wince. "She knows. Mother's coming for you. We have to go now."

I shook my head. "We can't. Aria—"

"You're not listening to me, Finn. She. Knows." Annabelle took my elbow, dragging me towards the door. It flew open again before we reached it.

Angelina stood in the doorway, two large, robed men behind her. She looked slowly from me to Annabelle, and then smiled, creepy and serene as ever. "Why doesn't it surprise me that you were involved?" she said to Annabelle. She looked back over her shoulder at the two men. "Take them both. Restrain them in the main courtyard."

"Wait, no!" I scrambled to get in front of Annabelle, but the men were already grabbing her. "It was me! Just me. Annabelle had nothing to do with it!"

How much did Mother know? That I planned to escape or that Aria was coming with me? Oh god, had she caught Carly?

"Leave her alone! It was all me."

Don't give specifics, I thought. *Take the blame, but don't let them goad you into giving them more ammunition.*

Tony. It had to be Tony. He'd blabbed to someone, who'd blabbed to someone else, all of them excited about leaving, until they told someone who wasn't. Someone who thought they should stay. Someone who told.

"Let Annabelle go! She did nothing. It was me!"

"Be silent," Angelina said. "Perhaps you should have listened the first time."

They dragged us out into the main yard, forcing us back-to-back against a pole. Annabelle grabbed my hand and squeezed it. The men took a roll of duct tape and wound it around the two of us, fixing us in place. At least it was just duct tape, not chains. Perhaps there was still a chance of getting free.

Around us, members of The Retreat stared. A few moved forward, as if to help us, or maybe to help restrain us, and were waved off by Angelina. And then I saw her. Lucy's mother, standing at the front of the crowd, watching. It wasn't Tony who had betrayed me; it was her.

"They killed her," I yelled. "They killed Lucy, and still you support them?"

She raised her chin, staring me down. "My daughter broke the rules. She had to be withdrawn. Mother makes the decisions that keep us safe."

I shook my head slowly. Was she really so indoctrinated that she didn't even care that her daughter was dead? My words had caused a stir in the crowd, though. Robed figures turned to each other, muttering softly.

"That's right – Mother killed Ada. You didn't know that's what she meant by *withdrawn*, did you? How many others have been taken away, never to return?"

"Mother has asked everyone to go inside," Angelina called over the top of me. "She will inform you when there is something you need to know."

People stared at each other, not moving. My words had had an impact. They had to have asked questions before this, surely? They must have wondered where people went – why they never came back.

They didn't know me; they didn't owe anything to me, but they had to have known Annabelle. She was so kind; I was sure she must have been well liked. They wouldn't let this happen to her, would they?

"Inside, everyone," Angelina said again, and this time the crowd did turn away.

"Wait!" I yelled, but Angelina and the men herded the others through the doors. A few looked back, but no one turned around.

"Dammit!" I screamed. I strained against the duct tape. I was stuck fast.

"Stay calm, Finn," Annabelle said. "It's going to be okay."

How? How was this going to be okay? I'd fucked up – again – and I'd dragged her into it with me. Her, and who else?

"Lucy – Ada – is dead," I said again. "They killed her."

I heard Annabelle swallow. "I know, Finn, but we have to stay calm."

"Why? What's the point?" I strained against the tape, feeling it cut into my arms.

"The point is, I think Mother is planning on publicly punishing us, maybe even withdrawing us, and we need to find a way out of this."

Well, that shut me up. I sank back against the pole, against Annabelle's shoulders. "How much does she know?"

Annabelle shook her head. "Just that you snuck out to see Ada. By inference though, she knows that you knew her, and were probably involved in her and Aria sneaking around after lights out."

That part was the death sentence. Anything else, I might have been able to get away with, but endangering Aria... that was unforgiveable in Mother's eyes.

"Think, Finn. Tell me everything you know. Anything that could be helpful."

Think, Finn. Breathe. Think it through. What do you know?

Annabelle's words were so close to my mother's, I could almost pretend it was her behind me, my mother's shoulders I was leaning against.

"Helpful how?"

"I don't know. We might have to talk – or fight – our way out of here. Anything you can think of that might help with either of those options."

I took a breath. "Carly's coming back today. She's going to try and bring the police – if they'll listen to her – and Aria's dad. And Carly's mums." Honestly, Carly's mums were probably the ones Mother should be most afraid of. They were as protective of me as of Carly, and the two of them would tear Mother to pieces if they could see us now.

"That's good. We just have to hold on until then. What else?"

"Aria is Mother's daughter, and Mother started calling me by her dead son's name."

Annabelle nodded slowly. "We might be able to use that. Anything else?"

"Lots of the kids here want to leave. Some of them asked to come with me."

"We can definitely use that. Good job, Finn."

It didn't feel like a good job. It felt like I'd created a massive mess she was now stuck in the middle of.

"Is the duct tape stuck to your skin?" I asked her.

Annabelle wriggled a little, as if assessing. "Just my robe, I think."

"Same." That was something. "Maybe we could squirm our way out of them?"

We both wriggled for a moment, and I had the most absurd flashback to being twelve, at the beach, trying to change into my swim trunks inside a towel. What the hell, brain? That was not a comparable emotional moment. This was life or death, that was just life or public nudity, though I'll admit, at the time it probably felt like the same thing.

I flopped back against the pole. "My arms are too tight against my sides," I told Annabelle. She nodded, her head knocking back against mine.

"Same."

We'd keep trying, of course, but I didn't hold out much hope that it would work.

"Will you be able to run?" I asked her. "If you get free, I mean?" The last few days, she'd barely been able to stand. Adrenaline was supposed to do amazing things. Hell, if it came down to it, maybe a life-or-death moment would mean I could pick her up and carry her, even with my broken wrist.

Annabelle was quiet for a long time. I'd expected her to say something positive, reassure me that she would do her damnedest to drag herself up and sprint if she had to. Instead, her voice was hesitant. "I'm not sure. I think I might be bleeding again."

Woah.

I tried to turn my head to look at her. We were stuck too tightly together.

"I think if it comes down to running, you might have to leave me," she said.

"Not happening."

"You're going to have to. And I'm telling you now, if you've got visions of sticking around here, trying to get Aria out, you're going to have to cut that out right now. No one except the police are going to be able to pry that girl from Mother's clutches, and even then..." Annabelle took a long breath.

I pressed my lips together, tight. She was right. Of course she was right, but it didn't make me any less pissed that she was saying it.

"I left my mum and my sister," I told her. "In the car accident that killed them. I thought I remembered her telling me to go get help – that I had to leave to save her and Joey. The last few months, I've been feeling like I killed her by going, but she was already dead. I left to save myself."

Something ran down my face. Tears. I was crying, yet again, as useless as that was. Carly was right. The report had said Mum and Joey died on impact, and I remembered their faces – cold and unmoving. I knew it was true, but I still felt like I'd betrayed them. I should have stayed with them, even if it meant dying too.

Annabelle tightened her grip on my hand. "We sedated your father because he kept crying out for Joey," she said. "He was crying out for you too, Finn. He hated being separated from you."

More tears fell at that. In the year since Mum and Joey died, I felt like my dad had disappeared. He didn't touch me, didn't make direct eye contact. He was there but wasn't.

"You saved *him* by getting out of that car, Finn. He was barely hanging on before he came here. Barely, but that little bit he was holding on to was for you."

Maybe she was right, but I hated him for not coping more than barely. I needed him. I needed him to look after me, and make me feel safe, and not by dragging me out to a cult in the middle of nowhere.

"We will get him out too, Finn. We just have to hold it together until the police come."

Dad needed proper help, and he wasn't going to get it here, especially if he became the father of the kid who got maimed or executed in front of everyone.

Come on, Carly, I said inside my head. We should have made a firmer plan – a time when she would come – but of course, it all depended on her being able to persuade the police there was a danger. They must know about this place, surely. As long as they thought everyone was there by choice, they'd have no cause to enter.

Carly could be convincing. She'd talked us both out of many a detention before, but this would be different. She'd be trying to convince a room full of cops that people at a camp in the middle of nowhere, which you only had GPS coordinates for, had just killed a thirteen-year-old girl and buried her out in the woods.

Oh god, I'd sent Carly to the police station with a box full of kittens, almost as if I'd been trying to make her seem delusional. She could still do it though, right? She could still get back here in time to stop Mother?

Panic tightened my throat. Mother wouldn't really kill us, would she? Two days ago, I would have said no, but after what happened with Lucy... That thought brought me up short. My brain hadn't fully wrapped itself around that part. Lucy was dead – actually dead – and maybe so were we. We were still here, in Schrödinger's box full of radioactive poison, alive and dead. Or maybe just dead.

"Do you have anything on you?" Annabelle asked. "Anything that could be useful?"

I dragged my thoughts back to her – back to being strapped to a pole in the middle of the yard. The robes didn't have pockets, but my boxers did. (I'd always found that weird. Who was going to go rooting around in their boxers for their keys or wallet? But right now, I could have kissed whoever sewed those little flaps of fabric.)

"A torch," I said. "Like a key ring one, and a key." I'd never got the stolen items back to the panel under Mother's seat. I also had my dead phone and the spoons in the makeshift splint Annabelle had made, but I doubted they'd be much use.

"Can you get the key out? Maybe you could use it to cut the duct tape?"

Maybe, but my arms were still stuck to my sides. It was better than doing nothing, though. "I'll try. You keep trying to get out of your robe."

The two of us resumed our wiggling. If I managed to shake the key free from my pocket, maybe I could pick it up through the robe. I jerked my hip, trying to tip my pocket sideways. The keys stuck fast.

"What do you think happens from here?" I asked.

Annabelle made a noise in her throat. "I don't know. I've never had anything to do with the withdrawals before. Honestly, I thought they just took them back into town on one of the supply trucks."

I shuddered at the memory of Lucy lying on the ground in the forest. "They kept Lucy out in the repercussion rooms for a few nights. Maybe they won't do anything to us today?"

"Maybe," Annabelle said, but there wasn't much conviction in her voice. The fact that we were strapped to a pole in the middle of the yard in full view of everyone didn't give the impression they were going to wait.

Just a few hours. If they just held off for a few hours, it would give Carly time. But even as I thought that, the doors opened, and Mother walked out. I cursed under my breath.

"Just stay calm, Finn. We can still figure this out."

Angelina and the two men who'd taped us up followed at Mother's heels, and behind them came the rest of The Retreat members. I mean, everyone. Hooded figure after hooded figure filed out into the yard, assembling in a circle around us. They weren't bringing the children out, thank goodness, but it looked like all of the adults and teens were coming. How many were on our side? How many wanted out? I searched for Tony's red hair in the crowd, but everyone kept their heads bent, muslin wraps drooped low to hide their faces.

That was something, wasn't it? If they were afraid to look at us, it meant they knew this was wrong. Only one pair of dark eyes met mine – Aria's.

She bit her lip, fear and guilt fighting for dominance in her expression, but the sight of her gave me hope. The doors to the health room opened, and figures came filing out of there too. That hope sank right back down again. My dad stumbled out, held up between two robed figures.

I looked back at Mother. She would use him against me. If I tried to run, she would hurt him in my place, I was sure of it.

"Stick to the plan, Finn," Annabelle whispered, but we had no plan. I'd never had a real plan. "If you get the chance, you have to run. That's the only way to get the rest of us out of here."

I didn't answer.

"Together we breathe; together we are safe," Mother called out.

"Together we breathe; together we are safe," the others chanted back. They all inhaled, and I found myself breathing in automatically.

"A few days ago, I told you that one of our members had been withdrawn," Mother said. Was it only a few days ago? That moment had been so intense. I remembered my nose-bleed, and the feeling of falling into the darkness.

Right then, I'd thought things were as bad as they could get. How wrong I'd been.

"I did not inform you at the time, of the reasons. Ada threatened the safety of our community – of one of my most precious children."

Angelina pushed Aria forward, and Mother grasped her hands, as if holding her up for The Retreat to see.

Aria shook her head. "It wasn't like that. I went with Ada willingly. It was my idea!"

Mother wasn't listening. "Last night, I learned that Ada did not act alone. These two helped her."

Gasps and mutters made their way around the group. I couldn't tell whose side the crowd were on. Some of them shifted their feet uncomfortably, as if uneasy with the direction this was taking, but others leaned in, eager. It was so hard to read them with the robes covering their faces. Hard, too, for them to read each other. The crowd shivered with tension; there were no cues for group-mentality to take hold of. That could be a good thing. I could still sway them.

"Her name was Lucy," I called out. "Not Ada. Lucy Rogan. She was thirteen years old, and Mother killed her."

A ripple went through the group, of shock, this time. On my side now, definitely.

"Mother killed her," I said again. "That's what she means by withdrawing someone, and that's what she's planning to do to us. She's going to kill us, here, now, in front of you."

The ripple became a wave, some of the group stepping back and others surging forward. Mother's henchmen stopped them. Another smaller circle of strong, robed figures closed in around Annabelle and me, protecting us from the crowd. No, not protecting us. Separating us from them.

Their backs were turned to us, and I shook my leg desperately, trying to free the key.

"Any luck getting out?" I called to Annabelle.

"Maybe," she said. "I think I can get my arm loose. Just keep talking."

Talking. I'd never been great at that because Carly always did it for me. I'd missed my chance anyway. Mother was already addressing the Retreaters.

"Everything I have ever done has been for your safety. You know this. This boy is a danger. He tricked me, purposefully reminded me of Aaron, purposely made me think my son had returned to me, and..." Her breath hitched.

More mutters from the crowd, the name Aaron being passed from mouth to mouth.

"I'm not Aaron," I said. "Aaron died. It was an accident. A senseless accident, just like my mum and my sister dying."

Aria's brow furrowed. There was too much that she didn't understand. She understood Mother planned to hurt me, though, and perhaps that would mean she would forgive me for what I was about to do.

"Your daughter is still here," I told Mother. "Aria is still here."

The small circle of men stirred at that. Even they hadn't known the full story, it seemed.

"I found her father, you know. He's coming here." God, I hoped he was coming. "You need to stop this."

Mother shook her head. "Lies. Don't you all see this? He's threatening our safety. He's—"

"*You* are threatening our safety!" Aria shouted.

Mother's mouth fell open. She turned slowly to face Aria, whose hood had fallen back. Her whole body shook as she stared at Mother, her eyes at once wild and intensely focused.

"I would never," Mother started. "Everything I have ever done was to—"

"Am I what he says I am? Your daugh—" Aria stumbled over the word.

I felt something sharp crack inside my chest. How sad that "daughter" was one of the words Mother's own child didn't know. How messed up that in trying to give this place a "Mother", she had deprived Aria of that very thing.

Mother stepped towards her. "You are my precious children," she said to Aria, and I finally understood. That plural – it wasn't about the other babies born here; it never had been. The other precious child was Aaron. She'd thought *I* was Aaron, because she thought if she made it safe enough, he would come home.

"And you are dangerous," Aria hissed.

Suddenly, the tension on the duct tape released. Annabelle scrambled up, clothed only in a slip, her robe still stuck to the pole behind me. Blood ran down her thigh, and she stood doubled over, her skin paling to grey.

"They're escaping!" Angelina yelled.

I hauled myself to my feet. The duct tape still tethered me to the pole. Aria ran towards me, and Mother yanked her back. I bent forward at the waist, throwing the robe up and off over my head. Where were the keys? They hadn't got me loose, but they'd still make a good weapon. Of course, they chose that moment to come free from my pocket, landing somewhere in the folds of my discarded robe.

"You see? They are dangerous," Mother said. "We must withdraw them – now – all of us, or they will destroy our safety."

Angelina picked up a rock. She ran towards us, raising it in her hand. I shoved Annabelle behind me, and struck out with my injured hand. Pain rolled down to my shoulder as my wrist connected with Angelina's temple. She stumbled back, clutching her head.

What the...? I glanced at my hand. She'd hit the spoons; Annabelle's improvised splint had become a wrist-mounted weapon.

"Danger!" Mother yelled. "We must stop them!" Mother picked up another rock. She looked around at the others, raising the stone in her hand. "Together we breathe; together we are safe," she yelled.

There was no responding call. People shifted. They looked at each other... and some of them began to pick up rocks.

"Oh god, they're going to stone us." Annabelle fell to her knees.

I went down with her. "Get up." I tried to haul her to her feet, but she sank down, dead weight. "Get up! We have to run."

"I can't, Finn. You have to leave me."

The people who'd picked up stones moved forward, raising them as they walked towards us. A kid dropped his hood and ran out in front of them to hold them back. Tony.

"Stop!" he yelled. "This isn't right – it isn't safe!"

He looked so small against all of them. They were still moving forward, rocks raised.

And then someone else was stumbling forward. "Finn," he yelled. "Finn!" His eyes were still cloudy, but for the first time in a long while, I saw my dad behind them. Aria broke away from Mother, joining Tony and my father in a pathetically small human blockade.

"You have to run," Annabelle said again. "Go!"

I'd left my mum and Joey because I had to, because they were already dead. It had haunted me, but it had been the right thing to do. I'd left Lucy because I hadn't known the danger. But I knew this time. Annabelle was still alive, and I would not leave her.

"Just stay down," I told her. I crouched over her and covered as much of her as I could. My splinted wrist became a shield over her head. A rock thumped to the ground beside her leg, and she screwed her eyes tightly closed.

More rocks hit us, and Aria screamed with each one. Mother walked towards me, slowly, that creepy, serene smile on her face. She hadn't thrown her rock; still held it clasped in her hand. "You understand, don't you? I have to keep her safe."

Aria's scream turned into one long howl. Mother raised the rock. I cowered over Annabelle, squeezing my eyes closed.

The blow never came.

The crowd fell quiet, and in their place, a siren wailed. I cracked my eyes open. Mother stood, frozen in front of me. Her hand was raised, the rock still in it. But she was looking up. Up at a man who held her wrist, stopping her from bringing it crashing down on my head. A man with intensely dark brown eyes, just like Aria's.

Epilogue

Dad didn't come home with me. A part of me knew he wouldn't be able to, but it was still a shock when Carly's mums put me in their car instead of his.

"He needs to stay at the hospital for a bit," one of the mums told me. Honestly, I don't know if I registered which one. Her mums' names were Andrea and Becca, but I've taken to calling Andrea "Drea". I've had enough of A-names to last a lifetime.

I was okay with Dad staying in the hospital. He needed help – that's why I relaxed when I first arrived at The Retreat, thinking someone else was going to take care of him. A part of me still feels guilty about that. I barely thought about him the whole time I was there, being so caught up in trying to get Aria out.

My therapist says guilt is an okay emotion to feel. Actually, she says all emotions are okay to feel. You just have to be careful about not letting any of them take over – not letting any of them distort what really happened. I'm getting better at that... at least, I think I am.

A lot of people from The Retreat had to stay at the hospital. I guess some of them didn't have homes to go back to anyway. Like Dad, they'd cut ties with their old lives and handed all their assets over to The Retreat. The police said they should be able to get Dad's money back. Honestly, I don't care about that part so much, and I suspect most of the people from The

Retreat won't either. As much as Annabelle said silence would help me process my grief, facing the real world will do it just as quickly. A lot of people at The Retreat had been running from their feelings for a very long time, and coming back is their chance to heal properly.

Lucy's mum had a complete breakdown. I swing between feeling devastated for her, and feeling incredibly angry at her for taking Lucy to The Retreat in the first place. I know it isn't fair to think like that, but I can't help it. I'm grieving my friend as she grieves her daughter. Perhaps I'm also projecting. I'm still mad at my own dad for taking me to The Retreat.

As for Mother, Angelina, and Mother's other henchmen? I don't know whether they're in a hospital or prison. I suspect Mother, at least, is somewhere that's a combination of both.

Aria's dad has filled in as many of the blanks as he can. Those online forums Mother spent time on after Aaron died were filled with people like her – people who were grieving, or otherwise unstable. They'd all had obsessions about the things that might harm them or their children. It had become an echo chamber of baseless ideas. Of course, it didn't seem like that to them. Over time, they'd become convinced that disconnecting from society was the only way to save themselves.

Aria's dad doesn't know exactly how they managed it, or how it grew from a small group into the community it had become by the time Dad and I arrived. He also doesn't know how they avoided being noticed for so long, especially when he was desperately searching for them. I had some ideas on that. I guessed it wouldn't be too hard if you knew the right people – someone with land off the grid, another with more money than sense, and a third with the political connections to make sure no one looked too closely at what was happening. And of course Mother, who was just damaged and just charismatic enough to make others follow her.

"What is it today?" Carly asked me.

We were sitting on her living room floor, playing with one of the kittens we'd rescued. Carly's mums had firmly vetoed the idea of all eight staying, but they said we could keep one. Carly named him "Safety" because she has a weird sense of humour that no one else gets. The rest went to a local pet rescue who will find them new homes. I couldn't bear to part with them completely, so I started volunteering there in the evenings. Maybe I hadn't given up on the idea of following in Mum's veterinarian footsteps after all.

We were waiting for Aria's dad to bring Aria over. It turned out he lived just one town north from us, and I'd spent most of the last few months in transit between the two places.

"Hard candy," I said. "Definitely a choking hazard."

Carly let out a puff of air and rolled her eyes. "You're so lame. You need to introduce her to laser tag, or bungy jumping, or—"

"One thing at a time, Carly Throw. A few months ago, she didn't even know how to sit on a chair."

Carly poked her tongue out at me, but she didn't protest further.

It turns out, the world is pretty overwhelming when you've been kept away from anything remotely dangerous. I suspect the world is pretty overwhelming when your mother tries to kill people in front of you, whether or not you've been kept away from it. Aria was doing okay... or as okay as could be expected.

We'd come up with a system. Her dad and I would each introduce her to one new thing a week. So far, I'd mostly picked fun things – like hard candy – but we're going to do the not so fun stuff as well. She wanted to see the ugly parts of life too.

Carly and her mums were also teaching her about the things I couldn't. Carly insisted on that when I told her Aria had taken off her clothes the first time we met.

"When do you think you'll introduce her to movies?" Carly asked. "There are so many she needs to see."

Aria loved photographs, especially when her dad showed her pictures of Aaron, but she found TV overwhelming. She loved stories, though, so I thought she'd probably be delighted by movies once she got used to the fast-moving images... if we taught her enough that she could understand any of the plots.

I didn't think Carly would be satisfied with that answer. "Soon," I said instead. "Hard candy today, though."

A soft knock sounded on the door, still gentle and serene, old habits running hard. Perhaps next week, I'd teach her about something loud, though she'd already met Carly, and you didn't get much louder than that.

"Come in!" Carly yelled, as if to prove my point.

Aria opened the door. I grinned as soon as I saw her, and her expression mirrored mine. Today, she wore a fluro-pink button-up shirt, and green leggings. It looked... awful, and great, and so her. Who she was becoming, I mean. She loved colours, and different shapes, but she always wore something green, because – as she told me – she didn't want to completely forget who she had been at The Retreat either.

She saw me looking and held out her arms. "You like it? Dad took me op-shopping again."

"I love it," I said at the same time as Carly said, "It's hideous."

Aria grinned, apparently pleased with both answers. I guess it was just great to have a choice, whether or not other people agreed with it.

"I've got some homework to do," Carly said. "I'll leave you two to it."

"Since when do you do homework?" I asked Carly.

Carly shrugged. "Since I'm trying to be subtle." She waved her hands around in an exaggerated version of jazz hands. "Look at all this subtleness." She gave me a wink and disappeared into her bedroom.

I turned to Aria. "What was that about?"

She shrugged – a habit she'd picked up from Carly. "Don't know. Can we go over to your house?"

I hesitated. I'd only got as far as sitting on my porch over at my place. Going inside, with Mum, Joey, and now Dad missing, felt too much. I could picture every inch of the living room, my room, their rooms – all of it – but seeing it for real felt too much.

"Just to the porch," Aria said. "I like the swing."

I smiled. "Okay." Taking her to the park had been one of my first new things. She laughed when she was playing on the swings, maybe for the first time since leaving The Retreat, and it instantly became her favourite activity. And mine. The porch swing was a lot more sedate, but I had to admit, I enjoyed the gentle sway of it too.

We settled down on either end of it, and I kicked my foot gently against the porch, setting it in motion.

"When do you think you'll go inside?" she asked me.

I shrugged. "I don't know. Soon."

"Maybe today?"

"Maybe today," I agreed. I'd said that every week, but maybe today I meant it.

"So, what's this week's new thing?" Aria asked me. She smiled, but the corners of her mouth didn't quite stretch out like they normally did. New things were fun, but still scary.

I pulled the tin of sweets from my pocket. "Hard candy," I said.

"Hard candy?"

I nodded. She frowned at me, dubious, but I opened the tin and held it out to her. "You suck on it. It's nice."

"They look like rocks," she said.

"It's cherry flavour," I told her.

She gingerly took a piece and popped it in her mouth. Her face brightened. "It's sweet," she said, then she made a face. "But it's not cherry flavoured."

I laughed. "That's another thing I'm introducing you to – artificial flavouring. Nothing tastes quite like its name, but we accept it anyway."

She frowned, and I could see a whole string of questions piling up behind her tongue, none of which I would have the answer to.

"But you like it?" I asked.

She nodded. "Can I have another one?"

I held out the tin. I kicked my foot against the porch again, pushing the swing back into a gentle rhythm. It was good to be home, even if I wasn't quite in it.

"Finn..."

"Hm?"

Aria didn't continue, and I turned to look at her. "What's up?"

She didn't meet my eye. "Why did you kiss me?"

I swallowed, a lump instantly forming in my throat. I knew she would bring it up eventually, but everything else had just been... That was a cop out. I should have brought it up myself.

When I didn't answer straight away, she continued. "Ada—" She cut herself off and shook her head. "*Lucy* told me what it was called, and Carly explained what it meant. I just wanted to know..." She trailed off, a blush creeping up her neck.

I swallowed again, but the lump in my throat wasn't going anywhere. "I kissed you because... I think you're amazing," I told her.

She looked up at me, her eyes curious rather than creeped out, so I kept going.

"That night when we snuck into Mother's office, and everything you did for the kittens, you were so brave, and clever, and resourceful despite where you grew up, and everything Mother kept from you."

Aria's lips twisted a little at the mention of Mother. She didn't seem upset by anything else I was saying, so I said the last part.

"And I thought you were beautiful. Absolutely beautiful. So, I kissed you." I felt weird saying that to her. I'd never said that to a girl I'd accidentally seen naked before – hell, I'd barely even said it to another girl before – and it suddenly felt weirdly vulnerable. For her and for me.

"So, you kissed me," she repeated.

I nodded.

"Do you want to kiss me again?"

I nodded again. "But only if you want me to." I hesitated. "Do... you want me to?"

She nodded.

"Okay then." I didn't lean over. Just because she said she wanted me to didn't mean she meant right then. Like everything, I needed to take this slow, not rush things...

But then she was sliding over in the seat, taking my arm and putting it around her shoulder. "I meant now, Finn."

"Oh."

And then she kissed me. She tasted of not-quite-cherry flavouring, but she also tasted the same as she had the night I first kissed her. Like fresh air and sun.

She pulled back, resting her forehead against mine. "You should go inside the house, Finn," she said.

I nodded. Not what I thought we'd talk about just after we kissed, but okay. "I will," I said. "Maybe today."

"Maybe today," she repeated.

"Did I ever explain Schrödinger's cat to you?" I asked.

She shook her head. She leaned back against my shoulder, and I rested my cheek against her temple. I opened my mouth to start an explanation and then shut it again. "You know what, never mind," I said.

Safety chose that moment to trot over from Carly's house, which was both ironic and a good distraction.

"Safety, come!" Aria said. She hadn't quite got a handle on the differences between cats and dogs yet. Safety came anyway. He jumped up, settling on her lap.

"I think he likes me," she said.

"Of course he does," I told her. "I like you too."

I wasn't avoiding telling her about Schrödinger because I was trying to shelter her from the dead-not-dead cat, and the weirdo who decided the idea of putting it in a box with poison was a normal thing to think about. Aria had seen far worse than that, and probably some things I didn't even know about yet.

The cat had been Dad's metaphor for The Retreat, and that dead-not-dead part of my life was over. Life was okay now – good – which meant the cat was very much alive, and I'd rather just leave it that way.

A Note from the Author

Thank you for reading *The Retreat*.

Did you enjoy this book? You can make a big difference. Reviews are the most powerful tool when it comes to getting attention for my books.

As an indie author, it can be hard to get my books into the hands of readers, but honest reviews help me do just that.

If you've enjoyed this book, I would be very grateful if you could spend just a few minutes leaving a review (it can be as short as you like.)

Thank you very much!

Want a free book?

Awoman finds a Death Curse symbol scratched into the soap scum around her sink. A young boy watches his family fall apart after the death of his father. A butterfly chrysalis hatches under the watchful eye of a hungry cat, and a teenage grim reaper's job is made harder by the boy who can see her.

Sad, poignant, and darkly funny tales about death. If you like unique points of view, heart-breaking moments, and a touch of black humour, then you'll love Helen Vivienne Fletcher's first short story collection, *Symbolic Death*.

Or get it for free when you sign up for Helen's newsletter at www.helenvfletcher.com.

Also by Helen

Young Adult Books

Broken Silence

Underwater

We All Fall

The Retreat

Reactive Magic Series

Reactive

Magnetic

Volatile

Explosive

Reactive Magic: The Complete Series

Familiar Magic Series

Familiars and Foes

Accidents and Apparitions (published in Jingle Spells)

Curses and Cousins

Children's Books

The Trespassers Club

There's No Such Thing As Humans

Aunt Kelly's Dog

Jenny No-Knickers

Do Fruit Worry About Getting Fat?

Jack's Books

Short Stories
Symbolic Death
Beside the River Styx
Find out more at www.helenvfletcher.com

Acknowledgements

This book was written thanks to the amazing generosity of the Michael King Writers Centre, who gave me the time and space to write with a Michael King Writers Residency. I cannot thank them enough.

Thank you also to Michele Powles, my housemate during the residency. I really appreciated the meal-time chats and mutual encouragement as we wrote until our fingers hurt.

Thank you to my wonderful editor, Sue Copsey, and to Anthony Fletcher and Robert Hurley for helping me dig myself out of the tech-related plot holes I'd written myself into.

Most of all thank you to everyone who reads my books and encourages me to keep writing them.

About the Author

Helen Vivienne Fletcher is a children's and young adult author, storyteller, and award-winning playwright. She has won and been shortlisted for numerous writing competitions including winning the Outstanding New Playwright Award at the Wellington Theatre Awards, making the shortlist for the Storylines Joy Cowley Award, and the finalist list for the Ngaio Marsh Best First Book Award.

Helen has worked in many jobs, doing everything from theatre stage management to phone counselling. She discovered her passion for writing for young people while working as a youth support worker, and now helps children find their own passion for storytelling through her work as a creative writing tutor.

She lives in Wellington with her disability assistance dog, Bindi, a playful Labrador who loves soft toys, cuddles, and can fit three tennis balls in her mouth at once.

Overall, Helen just loves telling stories and is always excited when people want to read or hear them.